Looking
for
Yesterday

Looking
for
Yesterday

Marcia Muller

GRAND CENTRAL
PUBLISHING

NEW YORK   BOSTON

Copyright © 2012 by Pronzini-Muller Family Trust

Grand Central Publishing
Hachette Book Group
237 Park Avenue
New York, NY 10017
www.HachetteBookGroup.com

Printed in the United States of America

RRD-C

First Edition: November 2012
10 9 8 7 6 5 4 3 2 1

Grand Central Publishing is a division of Hachette Book Group, Inc.
The Grand Central Publishing name and logo is a trademark of Hachette Book Group, Inc.

The Hachette Speakers Bureau provides a wide range of authors for speaking events. To find out more, go to www.hachettespeakersbureau.com or call (866) 376-6591.

The publisher is not responsible for websites (or their content) that are not owned by the publisher.

Library of Congress Cataloging-in-Publication Data

Muller, Marcia.
Looking for yesterday / Marcia Muller.
   p. cm.
ISBN 978-0-446-57335-1 (hardback)
1. McCone, Sharon (Fictitious character)—Fiction. 2. Women private investigators—California—Fiction. I. Title.
PS3563.U397L66 2012
813'.54—dc23
                    2012007239

For Dave Brandt
aka Rosco

Looking
for
Yesterday

LETTER TO SHARON McCONE FROM CAROLYN WARRICK, PROSPECTIVE CLIENT:

Dear Ms. McCone,

The world's forgotten me. No more mentions in the press. No requests for interviews. No photo ops. The websites are being taken down. I'm yesterday's news.

And I never got my message across.

Firearms. They should not—cannot—be allowed in the hands of the wrong persons.

I know the truth of that. Oh, yes, I know. I saw my four-year-old sister Marissa with the blood drained from her tiny face. Saw my nine-year-old brother Rob staring down in disbelief and horror at the gun he'd just accidentally fired.

And my best friend, Amelia, ripped and shattered by bullets on her living room floor.

When I was unjustly arrested for the crime, I thought I could make a difference. State my beliefs to the court and press, leave a legacy for all the countless victims of the indiscriminate sale of firearms.

Right from the beginning everything went wrong: People magazine didn't go into the issue and, adding insult to injury, they used a bad picture of me—dirty hair and crow's-feet and snarly lines around my mouth. Oprah and all the other talk shows turned me down. I guess they didn't consider a woman who supposedly killed her best friend in a hideous manner and then was acquitted an entertaining draw.

Now I have my opportunity: Greta Goldstein wants to coauthor a tell-all book with me, but Jill Starkey, that bitch who used to be with the Chronicle *and covered my trial, is writing one of her own and trying to block ours. Starkey has attacked me in her columns from the first, and now she's bound and determined to profit from a false accounting of the crime I didn't commit.*

Truth is, I feel cheated. I suffered all that pain, spent months in jail, endured that awful trial. I deserve to tell my story. Greta Goldstein's a best seller, and a profitable book would help me escape from my boring little job in the real-estate agency; my tiny, damp, behind-the-garage studio apartment in the outer Sunset district; the defection of my friends and family members. I want to set the record straight about the loss of Amelia and Jake.

Always those losses.

Amelia, my best friend, and Jake, my former lover. She: shot multiple times by, as they now say, a person or persons unknown. He: because he believed the police's original case and couldn't bear to lay eyes on me. He's as good as dead, as far as I'm concerned. I bet that after I was acquitted, he couldn't bear to look at his face in the mirror either. At least I hope so.

Am I bitter? Damned right I am. Am I going to do something about this empty, empty existence? I hope so. I am requesting that you reinvestigate my case. I know this is unusual, since I was acquitted, but surely you understand how public opinion often overrides the judgment of a jury of one's peers. If you would grant me the opportunity of a meeting with you, I would be extremely grateful.

Yours sincerely,
Carolyn Warrick

TUESDAY, JANUARY 3

10:00 a.m.

Already I was tired. These boxes: how had I accumulated all that stuff during the years my agency was located in the now-doomed Pier 24½? Cardboard cartons filled the floor space in my new office on the top story of the narrow blue house on Sly Lane, a short block above the Embarcadero, below Tel Hill and Coit Tower. I wanted to shove them down the chute to the incinerator and turn up the flames.

My office manager, Ted Smalley, had found the building shortly before the city's port commission served notice on us to vacate the pier. I'd been dubious about the new location at first, but the underground parking garage and elevator—the old-fashioned kind with a metal grille—had seduced me. And the view was superb, even better than that from the pier, because I was looking out over the Bay from a height of exactly 143 feet above sea level—a fact I wouldn't have known, except that Ted had been given a handheld altimeter for Christmas. It had become his constant companion so, as he put it, he would always know how high he was.

But all those attractions were nothing, compared to the building's unsavory past—

My intercom buzzed. I picked up, and Ted said, "Your new client's here. Carolyn Warrick."

I had a new client? For an instant it didn't compute. Then I remembered her letter, which I'd received nearly a week ago. It had intrigued me and I'd researched her case, which had only intrigued me more.

I said, "Show her to the elevator, please. And warn her about the mess up here."

"Roger, wilco."

With the acquisition of the altimeter, Ted had become fond of using aviation terms.

I stood up, brushed dust off my jeans and sweater, and went to the elevator. It began whining and clunking its way up—noises that still alarmed me, even though the brand-new inspection certificate mounted on its wall said it was good to go.

When it arrived and settled—bumping some—I opened the grille. A woman peered out at me, brow wrinkled, mouth turned down. She was about my height, five foot six, with blond hair pulled back from a heart-shaped face and twisted into a bun at the nape of her neck. Better dressed than I, in a dark green suede jacket, black pants, and black boots.

"Ms. McCone?" she asked.

"Please, call me Sharon." I extended my hand to her, mostly to keep her from tripping, since the elevator hadn't quite aligned itself with the floor. "And you're Carolyn Warrick."

"Caro." She followed me into the office, glancing around at the stacks of cartons.

I invited her to sit down, motioning at the pair of clients' chairs.

"Sorry about this—we've just moved."

She selected one and sat. I took the other. There are some clients who feel more comfortable with you across the desk from them in a position of authority. Others want you beside them, to be their friend and—possibly—confessor. I sensed Caro Warrick was one of the latter.

"What a wonderful view," she said tonelessly.

"Thank you. When I get these cartons unpacked, I hope to enjoy it. Now, what can I do for you?"

She drew a deep breath. "Of course, you've read my letter."

"I did, and I've refreshed my memory of your case on the Internet."

"I'm surprised you agreed to see me."

"Why?"

"Well, the details are pretty sordid. Supposedly killing my best friend over a man, trashing her apartment after she was dead, trying to kill him after he found her body."

"You were acquitted. And you can't be taken to court again—double jeopardy."

"Acquitted, yes. But the stigma is still affecting my life. Many people have doubts about the justness of the verdict. As I explained in my letter, I haven't been able to get a decent job or afford a decent place to live. My family and friends have deserted me. Apparently everyone needs more proof of my innocence than the opinion of a jury of my peers."

"And you want me to supply that proof."

"As I said, so I can make it public in the book I'm coauthoring with Greta Goldstein. And I need it done quickly: a local journalist who has a vendetta against me is writing her own book and trying to block publication of mine."

"I know of Greta Goldstein's true-crime works. And the local journalist is Jill Starkey?"

"Yes." Her mouth twisted as if she'd bitten down on something sour.

"I see." Jill Starkey, a former ultraconservative columnist for the *Chronicle*, had covered Warrick's trial; her reportage had been negatively, even viciously, slanted. "Why do you say she has a vendetta against you?"

"I've always been a staunch supporter of gun control. For years I worked as an assistant director of the San Francisco Violence Prevention Center, and I had a close connection to IANSA—the International Action Network on Small Arms. Jill Starkey is a vocal member of the NRA. At my trial I spoke in my own defense, citing my beliefs and work as a reason why I couldn't have shot my friend. May I ask you something?"

"Go ahead."

"What is your stance on gun control?"

Not an easy question to answer. "I own two guns—for professional reasons only. I have a carry permit, but the weapons stay locked up most of the time. I take practice at the range very seriously."

"In short, you're for responsible gun ownership."

"Yes."

"I'm afraid I'm rabidly against firearms—with just cause. My father owned guns and kept one loaded in his bedside table drawer. That's where my nine-year-old brother found it before he accidentally shot my four-year-old sister to death."

God. That would make a believer out of anyone.

"Would my position prejudice you against working on my behalf?" Caro Warrick asked.

"No. I've worked for all kinds of people whose beliefs differed from mine. "

"In what ways?"

"Politically, religiously, racially—you name it. I learned something from each of them. All of them, I hope, made me a more understanding individual. Besides, our views on gun control aren't as far apart as they might seem to you. I'm for strict licensing. The need to demonstrate a reason for possessing a weapon. Background checks. Required practice; I'm a pilot, and I have to fly so many hours a month to remain current."

Warrick still looked skeptical. "Have you ever killed a person, Ms. McCone?"

"I don't see as it's relevant to your case."

"That's a yes, then."

"Okay, yes. In defense of myself and others. The nightmares still plague me."

She nodded, apparently satisfied with my reply. "Will you take me on as a client? Help me end my own personal nightmares?"

I considered. The woman fascinated me; so did the

weapons issue. Also, I had too much time on my hands lately: My efficient staff had settled into our new offices and were proceeding with business as usual. Hy was traveling a lot among the various offices of the international executive protection firm he owned. Close friends were away on winter vacations. Hell, I hadn't even found a good book to read lately.

Instead of committing, I said, "Tell me your side of the story."

Three years ago last October, shortly before her twenty-sixth birthday, Warrick had discovered that her best friend, Amelia Bettencourt, was having an affair with her lover, Jake Green. She allegedly confronted Bettencourt at the latter's apartment on Nob Hill and, in the course of a violent argument, shot her twelve times. The crime scene, according to newspaper accounts, was chaotic—items of furniture and smaller objects smashed, walls sprayed with blood and other human matter, windows shattered by so many bullets that it indicated Warrick had reloaded her weapon—a nine-millimeter semiautomatic—and gone on venting her anger even after her friend was dead.

Jake Green was coming to pick up Amelia for a dinner date and heard the shots from the hallway. He rushed inside and discovered Amelia's body and was phoning 911 when someone stepped out of the shadows and fired on him. He dropped to the floor unhurt, and within seconds the intruder left the apartment.

Green immediately suspected Warrick was the killer—a suspicion he relayed to the investigating officers. They questioned her, and she claimed innocence, but two eye-witnesses said they'd seen her leaving Amelia's building earlier that evening. Bettencourt's family was prominent in city political circles, and Jake Green, an up-and-coming stockbroker with a large Montgomery Street firm, claimed he had never liked Warrick and was intent on revenge. Caro Warrick was indicted and in the spring the case went to trial.

Warrick's attorney was Ned Springer, a public defender with a degree from what many considered a diploma mill in Idaho and less than two years of trial experience. No one expected he would win such an open-and-shut case, which was perhaps why the prosecution was not as prepared as it should have been. In the course of the trial, Springer stressed Warrick's staunch aversion to firearms and advocacy of gun control, and also brought a number of inconsistencies to light.

The murder weapon was never found, and according to state records, Warrick had never bought or owned a gun, nor was she the type of woman who would have known how to acquire a Saturday night special. The presence of Warrick's fingerprints in Bettencourt's apartment proved nothing, because Warrick often visited there. Warrick, a real-estate saleswoman, had been showing a house in the Richmond district at a time that would have made it nearly impossible for her to have arrived at the Nob Hill building by the time of the murder. And no blood-spattered clothing or other evidence of the crime had turned up in her apartment in the Marina district. Plus Jake Green's obvious vengefulness worked against the prosecution.

Juries are notoriously unpredictable. Caro Warrick's had surprised many by exonerating her of her friend's murder. Now Caro wanted me to help exonerate her all over again.

I told her I'd think about it and get back to her within twenty-four hours. She asked about my fee and found it reasonable. After she left I ignored the unpacked boxes and returned to my desk, swiveling to look out at the rain-soaked waterfront.

Behind me the elevator's grille clattered and Ted—slender and wiry—came through the opening. He looked immaculate in his blue silk suit—his latest fashion statement—but his dark, thinning hair stood up in tufts as if it were undergoing replacement treatments. I'd known Ted for many years, ever since I'd gone to All Souls Law Cooperative on an interview for its investigator's position and his big, bare feet had confronted me from behind the receptionist's desk. Over the years he'd changed fashion statements nearly as often as most people change their clothes; this latest was the best yet, but I doubted it would last.

"Lunchtime!" he announced.

"I thought I'd send out for a sandwich—"

"No way. You're going to have a decent meal for a change. You always cut corners in the food department when Hy's away."

My husband's and my schedules frequently didn't mesh: he traveled a lot; I was usually bound to my offices here in the city, but—wouldn't you know it—when a case took me out of town, I frequently missed his time there.

Defensively I said, "We've been busy with the move, so I haven't gone out much, but I eat at home—"

"You nuke stuff when Hy's gone; there's a difference."

I sighed, looked at the cartons of books, and gave in. "Where do you want to go?"

"Delancey Street?" The restaurant run by an organization of former addicts, criminals, and other disenfranchised people who had banded together to turn their lives around. Good food, reasonable prices, and not too far away on the Embarcadero.

"You paying?" I asked.

"As a matter of fact, I am. This isn't about business—it's about keeping you healthy."

1:00 p.m.

Rain spattered against the window next to our table. I looked out at it glumly; it seemed winter would never end. Of course, it wasn't the kind of winter they'd been having in the storm-battered Eastern and Midwestern parts of the country, but as a native Californian I expected better than this. Oh well, the snowpack was up in the Sierras, the skiers were happy, and we wouldn't have to worry about a drought—this year, anyway.

Ted said, "You're so down lately."

"It's January, Hy's gone a lot, and this morning I had a somewhat depressing new-client meeting."

"Carolyn Warrick."

"Right." I related Warrick's story.

"You taking her on?"

"I told her I'd have to think about it. It'd be a challenge, but..."

"What?"

"I'm not sure it's the kind of challenge I need right now."

"Why?"

"Because it promises to be major, and you know I've dealt with too many other major—and personal—cases in the past few years." My half brother Darcy's disappearance. My friend Piper's kidnapping. Others just as intense.

"But this one wouldn't be personal."

"Not at the beginning. But when did you ever know me not to get personally involved with anything more than a routine skip trace?"

"Never. But that's your nature."

"Maybe I'm sick and tired of my nature."

Ted just smiled and forked up what was left of his caramel cheesecake.

5:40 p.m.

My nature. My goddamn nature.

The narrow blue building was silent, except for the pattering of rain on the mansard roof above my fourth-story office and the humming of the remarkably efficient furnace. At the pier the rain would have been banging off the tin roof, the cars rumbling on the span of the Bay Bridge overhead. I'd've been freezing cold from the wind blowing through the dilapidated structure. And yet I missed it.

Missed it in the way I missed my old MG that had broken down frequently.

I shelved the last carton of books, then sat down in my newly reupholstered chair by the window. The chair had followed me from a tiny office under the stairs of All Souls Legal Cooperative's Bernal Heights Victorian to a bigger office there, to the pier, and now to Sly Lane.

Always ratty, sometimes disguised under a hand-woven throw. But the throw had worn out, a spring in the seat had started protruding, and when it came time to move here, I'd decided the otherwise comfortable chair deserved a makeover. Now it was handsome in light brown leather, and I'd ordered a hassock to go with it.

Outside, the lights of lower Tel Hill and the Embarcadero shimmered through the raindrops on the glass; the palm trees that grew along the central greenbelt were great shadows, their trunks swaying, their fronds windtossed. The day's rain was now turning into a full-blown storm.

I told myself I should go home before it got any worse, but still I sat there. If I wasn't back by seven, one of the young women next door—whom I paid to house- and cat-sit—would go over to take in the mail and feed Alex and Jessie. Hy was busy in Boston this week. I had no responsibilities; even my daily paperwork was done. I also had nothing I wanted to do. So I sat and let myself become mesmerized by the lights and the rain.

And finally it came to me: I was waiting for my decision. Tell Caro Warrick I wouldn't take her case, or tell her I would.

Part of me resisted; I didn't particularly like the woman, didn't understand her need to be vindicated again. But then I remembered Bobby Foster, a young black man on San Quentin's death row, whom I'd exonerated of the murder for which he'd been convicted. Bobby's trial had been a gross miscarriage of justice, based on a false confession—which he'd later retracted—induced by a lack of sleep and food and by police coercion. Apparently Caro Warrick's indictment had been another such miscarriage. Bobby had been fortunate to have out-of-state family members who would take him in after his release, so he could get an education in a place where his alleged crime was unknown. Caro hadn't possessed that luxury. If this book with Greta Goldstein could change her life, why should I deny her my aid based on a negative first impression?

8:15 p.m.

Warrick lived in an apartment behind the garage of a modest pale green stucco house on Forty-Fourth Avenue, a block from the L Taraval streetcar line. A cracked concrete walkway led between the house's right side and a newish redwood fence. Rainwater sluiced off the house's roof and splashed onto my hat—clogged downspouts, no doubt. I followed a shaft of light to Warrick's door. When she opened it, the odor of an aromatic candle, underscored by mildew, dilated my nostrils.

She took my hat and raincoat, shook them out, and hung them on a hall tree. Urged me toward a sofa. After I sat she went off behind a faded blue curtain that masked a kitchenette to make us tea. I took the opportunity to look around.

The ceiling was water-stained, the walls victims of bad patch jobs. But the Oriental rugs were of good quality, the sofa and chairs somewhat worn but durable. A flat-screen TV—maybe thirty-five inches—dominated one wall, and art glass knickknacks were positioned on the end tables. When Warrick returned she carried a silver tray containing a blue Wedgwood tea set.

She might have been living in a damp garage apartment, but her possessions affirmed that she had once been an affluent woman.

"I'm so glad you've agreed to take my case," she said as she poured.

"Before we proceed, I'll need your signature on our standard contract." I handed her the document I'd drawn up before leaving the office.

She read it over, signed it, said she'd give me a cashier's check for the retainer the next day. I put the contract into my bag, then took a piece of lemon from a little plate and squeezed it into my cup. I don't really care for tea unless it's iced, but lemon makes it palatable.

"Do you mind if I record our conversation?" I asked.

"Of course not."

I set my voice-activated machine on the table between us. "First I'd like some background about your life before the murder. Where you were born, how you grew up, that sort of thing."

"I'm sure that's all on record."

"But not in your own words."

"I see." She looked down at her folded hands for a moment. "I was born here in the city. At home, in the big house my parents used to own in the Marina. They had to sell it to help pay for my defense—even public defenders run up expenses. Now they live down the Peninsula in a tacky apartment complex in Millbrae and don't speak to me. Neither does my brother Rob or my sister Patty. They blame me for their losing the family fortune—such as it was. It's not fair: I didn't ask my parents for financial help."

She looked at me as if she wanted some sort of approval. I nodded. "Go on."

"Well, as I said, we lived in the Marina. I was the second child. We all got along pretty well—no sibling rivalries, no parental neglect or conflict. But then my older brother Rob accidentally shot our baby sister, Marissa. After that Mom and Dad were guilt-ridden and pulled away from us and each other."

"Did they become abusive?"

"No. We weren't that kind of family. Everybody just wanted the…incident to never have happened. We hardly even mentioned Marissa after the funeral. Mom and Dad threw themselves into their careers—she as an interior decorator, he as a financial planner. We kids threw ourselves into our schoolwork. Rob and Patty went to public schools, but after sixth grade I went to a private one—Miss Harrison's. I had special needs."

"Such as?"

"I'm dyslexic. And I used to have seizures."

"Do you know what caused them?"

"None of the doctors could figure it out."

"You say you used to. When did they stop?"

"I'm not sure. They just…stopped. One day I realized I hadn't had one in quite a while."

"How old were you then?"

"Nineteen? Twenty? Somewhere around that age."

"So after Miss Harrison's…?"

"I went to City College for a year, but I wasn't much of a student. After that I worked as a model through the Ames Agency. Did a lot of ads for Macy's. Maybe you saw them?"

I didn't remember them, but I nodded.

"That was where I met Amelia. She modeled too. Not because she needed the money, but because she enjoyed seeing her picture in the paper and on billboards. She'd just gotten her first TV work when she…died."

"Your relationship with Amelia—how would you describe it?"

"Close girlfriends. We'd go clubbing together, pick up guys. Do other silly stuff—you know."

"Such as?"

"Take the last ferry to Sausalito and sleep on the dock until morning. Roller-skate around the neighborhood in the middle of the night. Go looking for the best margaritas in the Bay Area."

I smiled, thinking of a long ago Best Ramos Fizz Hunt.

"And Jake? How did he figure in all of this?"

"I met him at a club in the Mission, the Screaming Eagle. After he and I got together, Amelia's and my friendship sort of slacked off. Oh, we'd still have drinks and talk on the phone a lot, but it wasn't the same. She resented Jake, and eventually she set about taking him away from me. Succeeded, too."

"And what was your reaction?"

"I didn't kill her."

"What *did* you do?"

"Tried to kill myself. Pills and booze one night. My sister Patty found me and I ended up getting my stomach pumped. Believe me, I'd never go through that again."

"I would hope not."

"Thing is, I was there that night. I *did* confront Amelia about Jake. She laughed at me, said he wasn't so great a catch and when she was done with him she'd throw him back. I loved him, couldn't stand her disparaging him like that. So I left in a rage. That was when the witnesses saw me in the elevator and the lobby."

"Did you go home?"

"No. I was a real-estate agent, had a house to show in the Richmond. I'm afraid I didn't do much of a selling job. Afterward I'm not sure where I went. It's a blur. All I can remember is flashes of purple and red and yellow. A blur of people. Fragments of music and noise."

"Perhaps you had a recurrence of the epilepsy?"

"I don't think so. There's an aura when an attack is coming on; I would've known what was happening. And if I'd had a spell people would've seen me, called 911. No, I have a sense I wandered the streets for quite a while."

"Where?"

She shrugged. "I don't know. It's one of those memories that's locked down deep. I've even tried hypnotherapy, but I just can't bring it to the surface."

When we'd talked earlier she'd seemed strong and in control; now she was fragile, vulnerable.

She said, "It's not going to be easy, is it—investigating for me?"

"No, it isn't."

"Are there any rules?"

"Only one: you tell me the truth at all times. If I find out you've lied to me, I'll terminate the investigation—and you'll forfeit the unused portion of the retainer."

"Agreed."

"Good. Now let's get to work. Tell me about your collaborative book with Greta Goldstein."

"She approached me last August. You know she's done a number of biographies and true-crime accounts?"

"I'm familiar with her work." In fact, Goldstein had approached me about a book on several of my cases. I'd turned her down; I didn't need or want that kind of sensational publicity.

"Greta's New York publisher, Wyatt House, was interested in the book. We signed a contract and started to work, putting together a timeline and establishing the major characters. Then in October, Greta's agent heard a rumor that another publisher had contracted for Jill Starkey's book and they were pressuring Wyatt House to drop us."

"Can they do that?"

"Anybody can do anything in publishing, according to

Greta. It's a tight-knit community: people owe other people favors, or have something on them."

Same as in my business—and the world at large.

"What was Wyatt House's reaction?"

"They stood by our contract. We'll deliver the final draft in April. In fact, I have to go to my self-storage unit in South City to look for a final batch of documents Greta needs. I'll see if I can dredge up something that might be helpful to you too."

"Good. And what about Starkey's book?"

"I hear she's having trouble with it. A lot of the people she needs to interview about me won't talk with her."

"This 'vendetta' you say Starkey has against you—could that be about your stance on gun control?"

"Yes."

"Nothing more personal?"

"We differ on issues—social, political, individual. Do you know Jill Starkey?"

"I've never met her and I don't read her column much."

"Then reserve your judgment till you talk with her in person."

11:50 p.m.

By the time I got home, I could already feel a psychic drain. This case was going to take its toll on me, that was for sure. The client was probably unstable, the details were sordid, and the outcome wouldn't matter legally. Yet I'd agreed. What the hell was *wrong* with me?

The house was cold; I turned up the thermostat as I went down the hall. The cats didn't come to greet me. I clicked on the overhead in the sitting room and started when a grunt of protest came from the couch.

"Jesus, you really know how to wake a girl up!"

My niece Jamie, middle child from my sister Charlene's marriage to country music star Ricky Savage.

"What're you doing here?" I asked.

She uncoiled her long, slender legs, pushed back the rich chestnut hair she'd inherited from her father. Screwed up her oval face in a scowl so like her mother's that I laughed.

The scowl grew deeper. "Please, turn that thing down," she commanded.

I hit the dimmer, went around the couch and sat down on the edge of the coffee table. "So to what do I owe this pleasure?"

"I'm up here on a gig. The first on a West Coast tour."

"You're performing?"

She sat up, pulling her feet under her and clasping her arms around her knees. "I've been doing these singing gigs around San Luis, you know?"

It was the first I'd heard of it, but I nodded.

"Different bands. Nobody big. But this one group— Cash Only—got an agent who set them up with a tour, and they asked me to go along. Cal Poly isn't working out too well for me, so I said yes. And here I am."

"Why aren't you at your father's?"

"He's nervous about it, and he makes me nervous. He and Mom were really opposed to me dropping out to sing.

But that's because he knows how hard life on the road is. And Mom only wants me to get the degree because Dad got her pregnant when she was still in high school and she had to marry him and didn't get her GED or go to college until years later."

"Valid reasons. Your dad wasn't always rich or famous. And your mom spent a lot of lean years with him when having a high school diploma would've helped her contribute to their income."

"My mom was only into having babies, and my dad was only into screwing groupies."

I closed my eyes. There was more than a grain of truth in what she said: Charlene had had their six children in short order, and had frequently lived off my parents—who themselves were not affluent—while Ricky was out on the road. Ricky's record with star fuckers was legendary. But then Charlene had discovered a talent for finance, gotten high school and college degrees, and left Ricky for an international financier who had been one of her visiting professors. And Ricky had fallen in love with my best friend and occasional operative Rae Kelleher, married her, and turned into a totally committed man.

"Anyway," Jamie said, "eventually they came around to the concept that this is my choice and my life."

Good. My parents had thought I was wasting my— largely useless—degree in sociology from Cal by working as an investigator. My mother still complained that my job was too dangerous. But they'd also agreed it was my choice and my life.

"So everything's okay now?" I asked hopefully. Leaping

with both feet into a family conflict was not what I needed to do right then. Of course, neither was taking the Warrick case. But who ever said the events of your life will be opportune?

"Okay. Dad and Rae are coming to the concert in Berkeley tomorrow. You too, if you have time."

"We'll see, and you and I will talk more in the morning."

I tucked a soft blue blanket around her and went to bed.

WEDNESDAY, JANUARY 4

After I fed the cats and turned on the coffeepot, I looked into the sitting room to see if I'd wakened Jamie. She and my blanket were gone.

Probably excited and off with her band members getting ready for their tour kickoff. She was one motivated young woman, and I hoped the Bay Area debut would go well.

But when I called Rae, I found all was not well in her household.

"Damn!" she said. "She and Ricky…had words last night, and she stormed out of here. Ricky's been frantic. I wish you'd called to let us know she was with you."

"I would have, but all she told me was that he made her nervous."

"Too much fatherly advice."

"You talk to him about that?"

"Afterward, yes. But you know me: I'm a cautious step-mother, and this is something that's clearly between Jamie and Ricky and Charlene."

Cautious stepmother: why the kids liked her and often confided in her rather than their parents.

"So Ricky's frantic. What's he doing about this?"

"I'm not sure. He had to leave for LA early this morning. By now he's probably contacted Charlene, his lawyer, our security firm, and—for all I know—the animal shelter." Rae sounded weary.

"Everything okay with you guys?"

"It's fine when it's just him and me. But when the rest of real life intrudes—you know."

I knew. Oh, yes, I knew.

Not that Hy and I had problems about family, but still real life intruded, our jobs keeping us apart. In the past three weeks we'd spent a total of six days together. Something had to change.

8:45 a.m.

Cash Only's tour schedule wasn't easy to access. The band didn't have a website, and the various search engines didn't recognize the name. When I got to the office, I turned the whole mess over to Mick—Jamie was his sister, let him deal with it.

Up on the fourth floor—uncluttered at last—I turned my attention to the Warrick case and made a list of people to interview: Caro's parents and siblings; the investigating officers on the SFPD; her attorney and the prosecutor; witness Jake Green; any relatives of Amelia Bettencourt; Jill Starkey; friends, employers, and acquaintances of all the principals in the case.

Caro's family would be hostile witnesses at best; I decided to save them for later. One of the investigating officers was dead, the other had retired and moved to Costa Rica. Star witness Jake Green, Caro's attorney Ned Springer, and the prosecutor were unavailable, so I left messages. Amelia Bettencourt's mother had died; her father lived in Pacific Grove, south of Monterey, but he didn't answer his phone. Friends, employers, and acquaintances were scattered or difficult to identify.

That left Jill Starkey. She had for years been a conservative op-ed columnist for the *Chronicle*, but had been fired in 2010 when the paper had to pay an undisclosed sum to an individual who had successfully sued her for libel. She was currently writing for a radical right-wing paper called *The Right Shoe*. As in "If the shoe fits…"

I decided to pay Starkey a visit.

10:30 a.m.

The Right Shoe's offices were on the top floor of an old three-story building on Market Street between Sixth and Seventh. It was a neighborhood in transition: upscale businesses and prosperous-looking people abounded, but so did cheap liquor stores, check-cashing outlets, and homeless people. Crime wasn't as rampant as it had once been, but that was due to the highly visible presence of cops on the beat. In the dark streets and alleys to either side, drugs were peddled and violent events happened with regularity.

As I walked along from where I'd left my car in the underground garage at UN Plaza, I saw a derelict sobbing into his beer can as a police officer leaned over him, and a woman sitting on a folding chair behind a TV tray, offering her poems for fifty cents apiece. Budget cuts on the state re-development program had seriously imperiled the scanty progress the city had made with this area and the homeless problem in the past decade.

I gave wide berth to a shouting sidewalk preacher dressed in dirty white robes. Avoided the clutching hands of a raggedy man in a ski cap. Ignored the pleas of a woman who sat on her blanket with two small children. God, where was my compassion?

Well, I'm a city dweller, and if I gave to everyone—genuine needy cases as well as hard-core pretenders—I'd've gone broke years ago. And I could spot the preten-ders: the sidewalk preacher probably took in more a day than most wage slaves; the man in the ski hat wore an expensive wristwatch; the small children were dressed in Oshkosh clothing and their mother wore a diamond ring.

On the other hand, the sobbing man was pleading with the cops to transport him to a rehab facility; the poetess behind the TV tray was enterprising and proud of her work. I risked half a buck and bought one.

> *The morning, like the dove*
> *Flies away*
> *And leaves me to face my tawdry day.*

Not bad. Not good, either.

The elevator in *The Right Shoe*'s building was creakier than the one in my new location, and filthy. Squashed cof-fee cups and beer cans, crumpled newspaper, and various substances whose origin I didn't care to contemplate covered its floor. The odor was of human waste. I tried not to breathe deeply as I rode upstairs.

The paper's offices had probably been remodeled in the 1940s: a high blond wood counter; worn and scuffed linoleum floors; pebbled glass doors, one of which was cracked in a sunburst pattern. The youngish man behind the counter had a bad case of acne and buckteeth. When I asked for Jill Starkey, he silently pointed to one of the doors off the waiting area.

I knocked, and a harsh voice yelled, "Go away!"

I knocked again. A rush of motion came from inside, and a woman with frizzy brown hair and an unpleasant twist to her garishly lipsticked red mouth stuck her head out and snarled, "What don't you understand about *go away*?"

"Very little." I edged around her into a small office crammed with bookcases and piles of paper on the floor. The desk's surface was buried in more piles.

Starkey stood by the door with her hands on her hips. From the photograph that had accompanied her column I'd always imagined her as a large woman, but she barely came up to my chin.

"All right, you're in here," she said. "What is it? A hot tip for me about what those liberal assholes at city hall are up to? I suppose you want to be paid, but let me tell you right up front—I don't pay my sources."

I took out my ID and showed it to her. She wasn't impressed.

"Oh yeah, I've heard of you. Important bleeding heart PI. Keep getting your name and face in the paper and on TV. Well, not in *my* paper, sister."

"That's a relief." I removed some books from the only visitors' chair and sat.

"Well, make yourself at home!"

"Thank you."

Starkey hesitated, then skirted the desk and sat down in her chair. "I get the feeling I'm stuck with you."

"For a while."

"So what is it?"

"You covered the Caro Warrick case."

"Bitch who murdered her best friend? You bet I did. What's your interest in the case? No, don't tell me. You're working for the anti-gun nut."

"Then you disagree with the jury's verdict of acquittal."

"Of course I do. The prosecution did a shitty job. And Warrick's attorney, Ned Springer—do you know him?"

"Not yet."

"Well, he had a reputation of not being able to find his ass with both hands, but he can be charming. He charmed that jury. Some say he charmed his client too."

"Charmed her?"

"Come on, McCone. Everybody knew he was screwing her."

In my experience, when a person says "everybody knew" it usually means one or two people suspected. I filed the rumor for further consideration.

"What about the prosecutor?" I asked.

"Overconfident. Unprepared. Harvard grad, but he's not going anyplace in this town."

"Will you give me an overview of the trial from your perspective? Then I won't disrupt your day any more."

Starkey tipped her desk chair back; I sensed she no

longer considered her day disrupted. Quickly she began to spew invective against Caro Warrick, the gun control movement, the American justice system, and the American people in general. On the sensitive recorder in my bag, I was taping her tirade, in case somehow, someday I could use it.

1:40 p.m.

I was thoroughly sick of Jill Starkey's sarcasm and vitriol by the time I left her office. The woman was steeped in negativity: Caro Warrick was "a bitch who should've gotten the death penalty"; her attorney, Ned Springer, was a "buffoon"; the prosecutor was "an incompetent Harvard snob"; Jake Green, Warrick's lover, was a "cheap gigolo." Even the victim, Amelia Bettencourt, was a "whore who deserved to be killed."

Starkey's diatribe on American society was even worse: most people were "semiliterate fools"; the president was a "fraud"; the Democrats had always "sucked"; the Republicans were "a bunch of rattlebrains who had better get their act together." And then there were California's governor and legislators....

I'd interrupted her at one point. "Is there anything you *do* like, Ms. Starkey?"

She blinked. "Well, I..."

"Small children, animals, ice cream?"

"Can't stand children or animals. Ice cream's okay."

God, the woman had thought the question was serious! The humorless: how did they survive? If you can't laugh—

particularly at yourself—life can be a grinding, dreary proposition.

Laughter—it's what keeps us sane.

2:50 p.m.

I was sitting in Ned Springer's waiting room leafing through a six-month-old copy of *California Law Review*, which seemed to be the only publication Caro's former attorney subscribed to. Springer was already twenty minutes late for our two thirty appointment. The only article that had caught my attention was on environmental issues, and it was dry and not all that interesting. Finally I set the magazine aside.

The law offices were in a seventies-style building in the Sunset district on Nineteenth Avenue near Ortega; it looked as if it should be—and probably once had been—a dental clinic. Springer had been there, according to his Internet listing, ever since he left the Public Defender's Office and went into private practice. From the looks of his waiting room—cheap, beat-up furniture, half-dead plants, and a scowly, unwelcoming receptionist—no wealthy or high-powered clients had lined up at his door.

It was five more minutes before the receptionist's phone buzzed. She said, "Yes, sir, I'll send her in." Then she glowered at me and jerked her head toward the inner door. "He's back."

The door opened into a short hallway, where a man in a tan suit stood. Ned Springer surprised me: because of his waiting room and his tardiness, I'd expected a harried, rumpled, unprosperous-looking individual, but he was well groomed and had a friendly smile and a good, strong handshake.

"I apologize for being late, Ms. McCone," he said. "I volunteer for a mentoring program, and one of my kids had a crisis."

"I know all about those," I replied, thinking of Jamie.

We went into his office and sat down. It wasn't large, but in contrast to Jill Starkey's, it was ordered. The spines of the law books on the shelves that took up two walls were neatly aligned, and the few items on his desk appeared to be in their proper places. Of course, it could have been that he seldom consulted the tomes or used his stapler, paperweights, or stamp and tape dispensers.

He said, "You told my secretary you want to speak with me about the Caro Warrick case. Attorney-client privilege—"

"Has been waived." I passed over a copy of the document Warrick had messengered to the pier that morning along with her retainer check.

He read it thoroughly. Springer was, I thought, what my friend and attorney Hank Zahn called a "belt-and-suspenders kind of guy," making sure all the loopholes were closed. It was a quality both Hank and I respected.

"May I keep this?" Springer asked.

"Please do."

"Why does Ms. Warrick want you to speak with me?"

"She's hired me to reinvestigate her case, to get the facts correct for a true-crime book she's cooperating on. What I'm mainly interested in is how the two of you interacted, your impressions of her and of her innocence or guilt."

"It sounds to me as if you're investigating your own client."

"At her request."

"That's bizarre. But then, Caro always was a little off center."

"In what way?"

"She went to extremes: she had to be the best at everything she did; she had to feel most passionately, act most forcefully, make the biggest impression on everyone. Very often she managed all of those things, but if not, it was cause for full-blown depression."

"It sounds as if you know her well."

"I do. We grew up on the same street in the Marina. We even dated a few times."

"You're aware of her history of unexplained seizures and dyslexia?"

"The dyslexia is real, and she's learned to handle it well. The seizures she manufactured herself to get attention. She never had epilepsy or any other disease that would have caused them."

"She claims she doesn't remember when the seizures stopped."

"Well, she's lying to you, probably in order to gain your sympathy. She knows exactly when the so-called seizures stopped—the day she started to throw one in her shrink's office, and he called her on it."

"She didn't mention having been under psychiatric care."

"This was nine or ten years ago, during her abortive attempt at college. It was fashionable at the time to be in therapy, but she probably needed it too."

"What was the psychiatrist's name?"

Springer thought a few seconds. "Richard Gosling. I think his offices are in 450 Sutter."

I noted the information; I'd need separate permission from Warrick to talk with her therapist, and I wasn't sure she'd consent to that.

I asked, "Will you describe what kind of client Caro Warrick was?"

"Passive and not very helpful with building her defense. She insisted upon her innocence and seemed to think her well-publicized stance on gun control would prove she never could have shot anyone. When I explained that many people go against their principles in times of stress, she simply said, 'I don't.' Fortunately there was no real evidence against her, so I was able to win an acquittal. She didn't seem to be particularly relieved or grateful."

"Yet now she wants that acquittal affirmed."

"You said it's a true-crime account she's hired you to gather background for?"

"That's right."

"Well, there you have it. Money. Money's been a primary motivation for Caro her whole life. The Warricks lived well, but not well enough for her. Her parents are still active and in good health, and besides, any inheritance from them would have had to split three ways. But Caro had big dreams. That was why she was so upset over losing Jake Green to Amelia; his family has multimillions, and he was about to come into a substantial trust fund."

"What were these big dreams?"

"Luxury homes and cars and yachts and travel. Expensive clothing and jewelry. Never having to work. You know, the usual."

I thought of Caro's dingy studio apartment, her boring little job. If she had a car, it was most likely old and badly used. No yacht, and she probably hadn't left the city since her trial. Such dreams die hard, but very few people kill for them.

Very few—but was Caro one of them?

4:15 p.m.

Back at my office, I returned a message from Rae. She said, "Jamie's been in touch. Mick tracked her down and made her phone us."

"Where is she?"

"Berkeley, with Cash Only. They're doing a gig at some place called the Damp Cellar tonight, and she asked me to be there. Mick and Alison are going too. You want to go with?"

"What time does it start?"

"Eight."

I considered. If I sent out for a sandwich and worked on my summary of the day's activities on the Warrick case, I could spare a few hours to watch my niece perform. "Why not?" I said. Besides, I might be able to get my blue blanket back from her.

THURSDAY, JANUARY 5

1:30 a.m.

The concert was a big success, even though the drummer later passed out in the band's van from too much beer and the bass player fell asleep at the table while we were celebrating.

"They do that all the time," Jamie told me as she—under the drinking age and thus the sober designated driver—steered her rental car over the Bay Bridge toward the city.

Mick said, "You need to get a better band."

"Believe me, I'm working on it."

I was the last to be dropped off. I hugged Jamie and started to get out of the car, but she twisted around and pulled a tote bag from the backseat.

"What's this?" I asked.

"Your blanket. You didn't think I'd steal it, did you?"

We both laughed, and I hugged her again before I got out and started up the front steps. The porch light had burned out a couple of days before, and I hadn't gotten around to replacing it, but Michelle Curley, my cat- and house-sitter, had left the hallway light on for me. Still, it was dark and I stumbled over something large and unyielding close to the door.

A person. On my front porch. One of the homeless street people?

Warily I reached over the person and unlocked the door, disarmed the security system, and looked down.

My God! Caro Warrick.

Her entire face was bloody, and there was a gash above her hairline that leaked.

She was bleeding, so still alive. I felt for a pulse anyway: barely there, no time to waste, not wise to move her.

I pulled my phone out and dialed 911, questions crowding my mind: Who had attacked her? Why? And why had she come to my house?

The night around me seemed colder, blacker. As I made my report to the dispatcher my gaze moved over the quiet street: few lights showed in the windows, and nothing moved. A shiver traveled along my spine. Whoever had attacked Caro could be watching from a short distance away, girding himself to also attack me....

I waited, vigilant. Traffic thrummed on the far-off freeways. A television flickered and mumbled in the house across the way. A car's brakes squealed on the cross street. My nerves tingled. Never again would I be immune to the fear of assaults in dark places.

After a few frozen moments I remembered the blue blanket Jamie had returned to me, took it from the tote bag, and spread it over Caro's still form. Checked her pulse again. Weaker.

Damn the slow emergency response time in this town!

I held Caro's hand tightly, spoke to her: "You'll be okay,

the paramedics are on the way. Everything's going to be all right."

The empty but comforting words we offer up to the sick and injured, even though, in our ignorance, we can't possibly know what the outcome will be.

While I held Caro's hand, I looked around for a weapon. I didn't see one, but there was a scattering of papers over the steps below. Also a badly torn eight-by-ten envelope with my name on it. The items Caro had said she'd search for in her storage locker? They looked as if her assailant had gone through them, maybe removed something. I gathered them up and put them in my bag; she'd intended them for me, and I wanted a look at what was left. If anything pertinent to this attack remained I'd turn it over to the investigating officers.

2:11 a.m.

Caro had been struck with a blunt instrument, an EMT told me; she had a concussion but that her condition didn't seem to be critical, though head wounds always bleed profusely. As she was being transferred to the ambulance, one of the cops found the blunt instrument, a hammer, on the ground beside my front steps. I wanted to ride along with Caro to the trauma unit at SF General, but a plainclothesman stopped me and asked me the same questions I'd already asked myself. I didn't have many answers for him either.

When the police finally left, I called the hospital and was told Caro's condition was stable. Then I sat down and read through the contents of the envelope I'd found. They were Xeroxes of newspaper clippings, and I couldn't find anything in them that I didn't already know. Maybe Caro's assailant had taken something incriminating to him or her. Or maybe I was just too damn tired to see what Caro had wanted me to.

I took a quick shower, set the coffeepot for six a.m., and went to bed.

5:32 a.m.

Someone was in the house.

I came awake quickly, heard steps approaching down the upper hallway—familiar steps. I relaxed, smiled, and closed my eyes. Let Hy surprise me.

He paused at the top of the spiral staircase that led down into our bedroom suite. His shoes clunked onto the floor. If he was trying not to bother me, he was doing a poor job of it. He came downstairs, and his clothing rustled as he took it off and dropped it onto one of the chairs by the small gas-log fireplace. When he slipped into bed beside me, I felt the heat of his body. Sighed and turned, pressing against him.

"You're early," I said.

"No, I'm late. Late getting here to be with you." He kissed me, long and deeply, then buried his face between my breasts.

Ah, homecomings…

7:15 a.m.

"You seem tense," Hy said, smoothing my hair and look-ing down into my eyes.

"I am. Something happened here last night." I told him about finding Caro's still body on the front steps.

His ruggedly handsome face and hazel eyes showed concern. "Why didn't you tell me when I got here?"

"I needed normalcy. Just us, and nothing ugly be-tween us."

"Understand." He put his arms around me and we lay for a while in the kind of peace we both craved.

After a while I said, "I need your help."

"You've got it."

"What d'you know about gun control?"

"A fair amount, but first I need some coffee."

"I set the pot on the timer last night. It's ready."

"I'll fetch it." He got out of bed, stretched, and went up the spiral staircase. I smiled, admiring the lines of his lean body.

A minute later he returned with two mugs, set them on the bedside tables, and crawled back in next to me, prop-ping himself on his pillows.

"Okay—gun control," he said. "It's a difficult issue. You know I wouldn't willingly part company with my guns be-cause of the kind of work I do, and also because I've had firearms since I was old enough to shoot. I enjoy and re-spect them. There've been times in my life when a gun made a difference. That ambush in the jungle clearing with the Cambodians. Crossing the Mexican border—if you hadn't shot that coyote who was after me, I'd be dead."

"But...?"

"Firearms aren't for everybody. Some people are careless with them, or just don't understand how to use them. Assault rifles are particularly dangerous. Who needs that kind of firepower outside a battle zone?"

"But how do you legally decide who should own a weapon and who shouldn't?"

"Congress has been debating that since 1934, when the first gun control measure was enacted. Constitutionality of withholding guns from what they call 'high-risk' individuals—mainly juveniles and convicted criminals—is another question. Then there's the problem of how to keep guns off the black market."

"Big problem," I said, thinking of a couple of pawnbrokers I knew who, for the right price, would procure and sell any kind of weapon to any individual who had ready cash. "The ATF can't seem to figure that one out. Neither can anybody else, for that matter."

"Right. Political divisiveness and the huge power of the NRA have pretty much created a stalemate. It all goes back to guns being made so damn attractive to the general public, especially to the young and impressionable. I blame TV and the movies for that. There's so much violence depicted that somehow it doesn't seem real. But you face down a fellow human being with a gun in your hand, it's as real as it gets. Well, I don't have to tell you that, McCone. It's a complicated world, and I've long ago given up on finding the answers."

I considered that for a moment. I'd given up on finding the answers to the big questions too. But the small ones— well, that was another story.

10:30 a.m.

I'd called the trauma center at SF General and been told by the nurse who answered—Amanda Lui, one of those who had attended me when I was in a locked-in state— that Caro had been put into a medically induced coma. She would rest peacefully until her concussion and head wounds could heal. Had her family been notified? I asked. She and others had tried, the nurse said, but no relative was available. I hung up and checked the phone book: Caro's brother, Rob Warrick, was listed at an address on Potrero Hill, not all that far from the hospital.

Rob's answering machine had one of those terse, slightly snotty messages: "You know what to do." I waited for the tone, but a man's voice came on. He sounded out of breath.

As it turned out, he didn't know what had happened to Caro, so I explained.

For someone estranged from his sister, he became ex- tremely agitated. "Oh shit! Nobody told me. My fault: I've been in and out and just got back from running. I haven't even checked my messages. You say she's in a coma?"

"Medically induced."

"What does that mean?"

"It's to make her rest until her injuries begin healing."

"How serious are they?"

"Pretty serious. But I think you should go over there, talk with her doctor."

"Of course. Right away. Oh, Caro…Is she going to die?"

"I don't know. How about you and I get together for

coffee afterward?" I asked. "I know a good place in the neighborhood."

11:25 a.m.

Mary Lou's Grounds for Divorce had been a Potrero Hill hangout for as long as I could remember, patronized by both medical personnel and local residents. It was said that Mary Lou Gould, a big, flamboyant redhead, had bought the place with the large cash settlement from her cheating doctor husband, but when asked about it she'd merely smile and put her finger to her lips. It was a small place with tables on the sidewalk, and I was lucky to snag one, this being one of those rare fine, warm January days that we sometimes enjoy in the city.

Rob Warrick—tall, blond, with the muscular definition of an athlete—was wearing shorts and a maroon T-shirt with blue stripes down the arms. His handsome face was pulled taut by worry lines as he sat down at my table and ordered a latte.

"I've just been to the hospital," he said. "They let me look in on Caro. God, she's so pale and still."

"Well, they did induce a coma—"

"Don't sugarcoat the situation. You know it's grim for her, and so do I. I talked with both the nurse and the doctor." He ran his hand through his longish hair. "Jesus, who would do a thing like that to her?"

"I thought you might have some idea."

"No. Oh, there are a lot of people who don't like her, because of her gun control stance or because they think her acquittal of Amelia's murder was a miscarriage of justice. But I doubt any of them are violent."

"You're in touch with Caro, then?"

"Of course. We're not close—Caro doesn't get close to anyone any more—but we see each other every few weeks."

"What about your other sister?"

"Patty? They got together occasionally. Why do you ask?"

"Caro told me she was estranged from her entire family."

Rob frowned. "Not from Patty and me. Our parents, yes. But neither of us sees them either." Something in his tone warned me against asking about the breakdown of relationships.

"*Are there any rules?*" Caro had asked when she hired me.

"*Only one: you tell me the truth at all times. If I find out you've lied to me, I'll terminate the investigation—and you'll forfeit the unused portion of the retainer.*"

"*Agreed.*"

My client had lied to me about being estranged from her family, as well as her alleged seizures. Should I allow her one more chance?

I asked Rob, "Do you know about the book on her case that Caro's coauthoring?"

"Yeah. I advised her against it. Bury the past, I said. But this Greta Goldstein got her really hyped up about setting the record straight in print. I wasn't at all surprised when Jill Starkey tried to beat them to the punch."

"You know Starkey?"

"I met her when she was covering Caro's trial. A real bitch, but I don't think she'd physically harm anyone. Caro didn't get that hit off of her, either, and she hasn't mentioned her since."

"What do you remember about Amelia Bettencourt's death?" I asked Rob.

"Very little. I was living in Manhattan then; my parents sent me east for prep school and then college and business school at Columbia." He added bitterly, "Getting me away from the scene of my crime."

"The accident with your little sister."

"That's a tactful way of phrasing it. I shot and killed Marissa. I was fooling around with my dad's gun and I pointed it at her, thinking it wasn't loaded. It went off—hair-trigger mechanism. I remember it every day, watching the life drain out of her. I tried to stop the blood with my shirt, but it was too late. I was such a fool."

"You were only a kid."

"But I knew enough about guns to check to see if it was loaded."

"You're being too hard on yourself."

"Someone has to be. My parents acted as if it had never happened at all. They shipped the reminder of her—me— off to school and never mentioned her again."

"And Caro?"

"She turned her anger against our dad. And got heavily into gun control."

"What's your stance on the issue?"

"After what I did, I think guns should be wiped off the face of the earth. Unfortunately, that isn't going to happen."

"What about Patty?"

"Patty? She's just sad. Sadder now that Caro's in the hospital. Patty's the saddest person I know. It's clinical depression, going back to childhood. I've tried to help her, persuaded her to get meds, but half the time she forgets to take them."

"Any chance she'd speak with me?"

"I can check and see."

Rob phoned Patty, who lived in the Rock Ridge district of Oakland. After a couple of minutes during which he kept saying, "Patty, don't cry," she told him she'd see me. She'd be in the garden; I could come over anytime.

2:10 p.m.

I'd recently read a magazine article about edible front yards—meaning you turned them into vegetable gardens, rather than planting a lawn or flowers. Patty Warrick apparently subscribed to the theory. Behind a low redwood fence, her yard was upturned in furrows, waiting to be planted. A few winter vegetables—brussels sprouts, chard, kale—thrived.

Patty, a large woman with long blond curls cascading from under a floppy-brimmed straw hat, was kneeling in the unplanted section pulling weeds. When she saw me she stood, her jeans smeared with mud.

"Welcome to my little acre," she called.

I stepped through the gate in the fence and surveyed Caro's sister. In spite of the cheerful greeting, I detected the flat toneless quality of the clinically depressed. Her eyes were puffy and bloodshot from crying. Wiping her hands on her jeans, Patty motioned me toward a deck that overlooked a side yard and what must have been an orchard, and we sat there on comfortable cushioned furniture.

"Can I get you anything?" she asked. "Coffee, a soft drink, some wine?"

"No, thank you. I'm good. What kind of trees are those?"

"Apple, pear, and plum. I tried cherry, but they don't do well in this climate."

"You're quite a gardener."

"A certified Master Gardener, with my own landscaping company. I love seeing things grow and thrive. But you're here to talk about my sister." Her voice grew even flatter. "I've been calling the hospital all day, but there's been no change."

I got straight to the point of my visit. "Caro told me you and Rob were estranged from her."

"Not so. She came to dinner here only a week ago."

"Why would she lie?"

"Because that's what she is—a liar. She can't help it. It's some sort of psychological condition."

"Related to the seizures she claims she had?"

"She's never had a seizure in her life, unless she wanted something. That's just the way Caro is. And neither Rob nor I is much of a prize, either. I blame it on our parents."

"Tell me about them."

"They're in denial, can't admit even to themselves that any of their children could be less than perfect. Their *three* children, mind you. To them, our little sister Marissa never existed. It's the only way they know how to cope with the accident. They travel around the world, never stay in one place very long. Pure escapism."

"Very differently from how Caro copes."

"Yes, and her way is a whole lot more sensible than my parents' denial or Rob's guilt or my grief. At least Caro wants to take positive steps: she went into high gear after the Gabrielle Giffords assassination attempt in Arizona, did some speaking engagements, but people kept raising the issue of the Bettencourt case. She withdrew and hasn't been active since." She looked pensive. "I used to be an activist for lesbian causes. Then, around the time of Caro's trial, everything inside me went flat. I just couldn't muster the energy...."

"That's natural after such an ordeal. What do you remember of the Bettencourt murder?"

Her gaze wavered and became unfocused. She might have been seeing either the orchard or some uncharted territory inside herself. After a few moments she said, "I remember Amelia; she and Caro were best friends. Jake Green I didn't like so much."

"What about Ned Springer?"

"Caro's attorney? He's all right. I've known him forever, since we were kids in the Marina."

"Tell me about Amelia. What was she like?"

"Pretty. Funny. Smart. She could be selfish at times, like Caro. She wanted what she wanted, and she made sure she got it. Especially men. Still, you couldn't dislike her on account of that. She charmed everybody."

"Including Jake Green, her best friend's lover."

"Especially him. He and Amelia were a good match; he was all about getting what he wanted too." Patty's lips tightened. "The first time Caro brought Jake to visit me—I was living in the Lake Merritt area then—I could see him sizing up everything in my house, putting a monetary value on it. From a few things my parents said, he did the same at their place. But then Caro introduced him to Amelia, a more lucrative catch, and he dumped Caro flat."

"Let's go back to the night Amelia was murdered. What do you remember?"

"I was at Caro's apartment in Cow Hollow. It was a tiny studio, very expensive, but she'd rented it to get away from Mom and Dad. She'd invited me for the weekend—a sisters' getaway—but then she got this phone call and said she had to go out. No explanation, nothing."

"When was that?"

"After we had dinner, around seven thirty. She came in sometime in the early morning and crawled into bed, drunk. I was pissed with her because it was supposed to be *our* night together."

"Did she give you an explanation then?"

"There wasn't time. The police came a few hours later and arrested her. I called Ned Springer and he represented her at the bail hearing the next day, but the judge ordered her held because she was a flight risk."

"And she never told you where she went or what she did?"

"Only what she testified to at her trial."

There was no way to phrase my next question tactfully, so I decided to be blunt. "In your opinion, could Caro have murdered Amelia?"

Patty didn't take offense. "Actually," she said, "I've always thought she did."

"Why?"

"No especial reason. Just a feeling. When she got into bed that night, she wasn't only drunk, but scared. The fear coming off her was as strong as the smell of alcohol."

3:30 p.m.

After I left Patty's I called the hospital for an update on Caro's condition. Still no change. Then I went looking for Jake Green.

According to the background information I had, Green had quit the stock brokerage and bought a travel agency south of the city in San Bruno. I called my own travel agent, Toni Alexander, and asked her if she knew of him.

"That little weasel?" she responded. "He tried to put the moves on me at the last American Society of Travel Agents convention."

"I take it you don't have a high opinion of him."

"It's not because he made a pass. I'm as open to that as any single gal. But he's just…ugh!" I could picture her shuddering.

"How so?"

"He's conniving. Petty crimes like selling for inflated prices the promotional flight coupons the airlines give out to those of us in the industry. Stolen tickets, too, when he can get his hands on them. And it doesn't help that he has eyes like a ferret."

I'd never gotten close enough to a ferret to look it in the eye, but I could imagine.

"Are you aware that Green was involved in a high-profile murder case three years ago?" I asked.

"Am I aware? He told me about it within three minutes of meeting me at an ASTA cocktail party here in the city. He was still 'jazzed' about it, he said."

"He give you any of the details?"

"No. I told him I'd heard about the case and escaped from his company—not very graciously."

"Good move."

"Not to change the subject, Shar," she said, changing the subject, "but have you and Hy talked any more about that trip to Tahiti?"

"We're thinking of making it a stopover on the way to New Zealand."

"I could send you some information—"

"I've already looked at stuff on the Internet."

"Shar, you're not really thinking of booking *online*?"

I had been, but I knew I wouldn't. Toni had done me too many favors over the years.

"Don't worry," I said, "you'll be hearing from me about making arrangements."

4:32 p.m.

More than two years earlier a Pacific Gas and Electric pipeline had ruptured down the Peninsula in San Bruno, creating a deafening roar that could be heard for many miles and a huge fireball that destroyed dozens of homes and killed several people. The commercial part of the city, where I was headed, had been spared, but grief, anger, lawsuits, and the eventual retirement of the utility's CEO followed. The disaster had made Bay Area residents very wary, and most of us checked carefully at the slightest whiff of natural gas.

All World Travel was located in a nondescript beige stucco building fronting an old shopping center on El Camino Real, the city's main drag. The small storefront was cramped, with two visitors' chairs and a table covered in brochures. Faded posters of exotic lands adorned the walls.

A young woman with long stringy hair who looked as if she'd like to be somewhere else was paging through a file at the reception desk.

Mr. Green, she said, wasn't in. If I wanted I could find him three doors down at the Reading Room.

"Reading Room?" I asked.

"It's a bar, his office away from the office." She snapped her gum for emphasis.

Classy operation.

You couldn't have read *anything* in the Reading Room. Its interior glowed a strange orange, broken only by the flickering of a big-screen TV. A hockey game was on, but the picture was so blurred I couldn't tell who was playing. At the bar a lone man hunched over a mug of dark beer. His hair was brown, and he had a perfectly round bald place on the top of his head.

I slipped onto the stool next to him, said, "Jake Green?"

He glanced at me, then looked away. His features were familiar from my files, but now fleshy and bloated.

"Mr. Green..."

"If you're a bill collector, go away. I've only got twenty bucks on me, and that's my drinking money."

"I'm not a bill collector."

"Then I don't care who you are. Go away."

I slid one of my cards in front of him. "Caro Warrick has hired me to look into the death of Amelia Bettencourt."

He glanced at the card, shrugged. "I'm done with all of that. She got her acquittal, what more does she want?"

"She's coauthoring a book on the crime—"

"Oh, shit, just what I need. Spread my name around, wreck whatever little I got built up here. You think it was easy, all that publicity? You think I *liked* having my face in the tabloids? All I ever wanted was a quiet, comfortable life. And I was on my way to having it, too. But the notoriety—my clients defected, I became nonproductive to the brokerage, so I bought the travel agency. Now the economy's in the pits, and whoever's traveling—mostly businesspeople—goes on the cheap. And there's the Internet...."

"That's a real run of bad luck. Especially losing Amelia. You were there that night. You found Amelia's body and someone shot at you too. I know it must've been very difficult—"

"Damn straight! One day I had a pretty good life, solid prospects, and the next day they're gone, all gone." He paused, apparently listening to echoes of what he'd just said. "Oh, God. Why can't Caro let it alone?"

"Did you know Ms. Warrick is in the hospital?"

His startled expression indicated he hadn't. "How come?"

"Someone beat her, probably with a hammer. She's in a coma."

"A hammer? Christ! Well, it wasn't me."

Too quick to spring to your own defense, buddy.

"I'm thinking it must've been somebody who didn't want her to coauthor that book," I said. "You have any idea who that might be?"

"Pretty much anybody who was involved with the murder. Maybe somebody with something to hide."

"Such as?"

"Well, the person who really killed Amelia."

"You were the one who directed suspicion at Ms. Warrick in the first place."

"Yeah, well, I've had time to think on that."

"To what conclusion?"

"Why don't you talk to her parents?" And that was all he'd say on the subject.

6:45 p.m.

The Warricks didn't answer their phone, and I didn't want to leave a message on the machine that would give them time to invent an excuse not to see me. Just as well—Hy and I had planned a quiet dinner for two at a favorite Czech restaurant in our neighborhood. At a little past eight, over chicken paprikash we talked of his travels and my doings since he'd left for Europe, talk that included work, but none of the specifics. Both RI and McCone Investigations had strict confidentiality rules—even between the respective owners.

Over coffee and brandy he took my hand and asked, "You thought any more about my proposition?"

Last September he'd suggested we merge our businesses. The benefits to me were great: it would give me access to a worldwide network of offices and operatives, and attract a larger and more lucrative clientele. Plus give me half ownership of a fleet of pretty slick jets. But I still had my doubts about ceding absolute control over McCone Investigations, even to Hy, and I wasn't sure that a high-powered executive protection firm was a good fit with our personalized service.

Now I reiterated those doubts to him.

"We discussed all that before," he said. "A merger wouldn't mean either firm would lose its autonomy, but it would allow us to tap into each other's resources more easily. And we'd enjoy better tax breaks."

Tax breaks. The holy grail of American corporations.

"And," he added, "we wouldn't have to hold these dinner conversations where neither of us can tell the other exactly what's going on."

That remark tipped the scales slightly in his favor.

"What would we call the company?" I asked.

"I haven't gotten that far in my thinking."

"Would we need to combine offices?"

"Well, McCone Investigations would become the primary US division, and RI would deal with international clients, so that probably wouldn't matter. But close proximity would be advantageous."

I thought of the little blue building on Sly Lane, where I'd only just gotten settled down. RI clients weren't likely to appreciate such casual quarters; we'd have to move again.

Hy saw the doubt in my eyes and squeezed my hand.

"We don't have to decide anything right away. Just keep in mind that we'd get to spend more time together. Work together."

"That I'd like."

"Then give it some serious thought. No hurry, no pressure."

My phone rang before I could reply: the floor nurse at SF General's trauma unit. Caro Warrick had just died from a cerebral hemorrhage.

"Have you contacted her family?" I asked the nurse.

"Her brother and sister have been contacted. The parents aren't available."

I thanked her and broke the connection. Said to Hy, "It's a case for Homicide now. And I've lost a client. She lied to me, she was a seriously disturbed individual, but in an odd way I liked her."

"How so?"

"Well, she'd been through a lot, but until recently she'd stood up for her convictions on gun control. I sensed something had spooked her, made her back off. She seemed afraid of something or somebody. Damn! I should've questioned her more closely."

"Case closed, McCone. Let's talk about us now."

"Let's."

Right—case closed. Or so I thought at the time.

FRIDAY, JANUARY 6

Apparently I was still employed, however. My cell vibrated as I was pulling into my assigned parking space in the underground garage at the blue building. A male voice asked that I hold for Greta Goldstein.

Who? Oh, yes, Caro's coauthor on the true-crime book.

Goldstein came on the line, her voice thick with a native New Yorker's accent. "Ms. McCone," she said, "I spoke with the late Caro Warrick recently. She told me you'd agreed to conduct an investigation for her."

"Yes, that's right."

"Have you had any success so far?"

"I've learned a few things that didn't come up at Ms. Warrick's trial, but I'm afraid I can't discuss them. Even though my client is dead, I'm still bound by the rules of confidentiality."

"Well, my publisher, Wyatt House, and I want you to go on with the investigation. This book is going to be written, especially now that someone seems to have gone to the ultimate to prevent it."

"You think the book is the reason she was attacked?"

"I suspect so."

"Do you have authorization to hire me?"

"Yes—a firm contract giving us the rights to reassign any investigative work in the event of her incapacity or death."

So I was right: Caro *had* been afraid of something happening to her.

"What about her family or heirs?"

"I've already spoken with her brother and sister: they have no objections. I understand her parents may not like it, but they're not party to the contract. As for her heirs, I doubt the gun control organizations she left the bulk of her money to will object to having the truth revealed."

"Her death is now an official murder investigation. I'd have to clear my work with the SFPD."

Goldstein laughed harshly. "If they're anything like the NYPD, they'll be delighted to share the case with you."

"True enough."

"Do we have a deal?"

"I'll have to check with someone at the police department, but yes, I don't see why not."

"Same terms as your contract with Ms. Warrick?"

"Yes."

"Good. Draw up a new one with Wyatt House as the client, and e-mail it to me." She gave me her e-mail address and hung up. No nonsense with this woman. No grief at the loss of her author, either.

I phoned the SFPD and asked who was handling the Warrick murder.

Inspector Devlin Fast. Did I wish to be transferred to him? Yes.

I knew Fast: he was tough-talking but fair and willing to cooperate with the private sector. A son of the Hunters Point ghetto, he'd graduated the police academy first in his class and risen to the elite Homicide squad in record time. It turned out he wasn't available, but I left a message on his voice mail.

Next I called for Mick to come to my office, and gave him a list of people to run deep background checks on: Jake Green, the witnesses and jurors at Caro's trial, Jill Starkey, even Ned Springer. The prosecutor, and Caro's therapist Richard Gosling. In short, anyone who had even had a remote connection with her during the time since Amelia Bettencourt was murdered.

"Tall order, Shar," he said. "Derek's caught up on a big fraud project for Thelia, and I—"

"I understand. Do whatever you can. Give it to me in bits and pieces."

After I'd gone over and signed a few more bits of correspondence I took the little elevator down to the first floor. Kendra Williams, Ted's assistant and our temporary receptionist until we could find a good new hire, wasn't at her desk. I skirted it and went into his office.

When he heard me come in, Ted stood. He wore another new silk suit, his tie loose at the neck and rumpled. Like the suit it was blue, but covered with small pinkish splotches that, upon closer inspection, turned out to be mermaids.

He saw me frowning at the tie and said, "A Christmas gift from Neal. He's got weird taste. It's the first time I've had the nerve to wear it."

Usually his life partner's taste was impeccable. I peered

again at the mermaids. They were carefully rendered, right down to the smallest scale and largest tit.

"A joke?" I asked.

"I hope. There was a gleam of sadistic satisfaction in his eyes when he saw I had it on this morning."

"Mmmm." I sat down on the edge of the desk.

"What's happening?" he asked. "You didn't come down here to check on my attire."

"We need a new contract in the Warrick case. Wyatt House, the publisher."

"Will do." He scribbled down the details I gave him.

I remained where I was when he was finished.

Ted said, "I promise I won't wear any more faggy ties to the office."

"I don't care if you go around in drag. I have a question for you."

"Yes?"

"What would you think of us merging with RI?"

He sat down heavily. "When did this come up?"

"Well, Hy mentioned it in the fall, but he let the subject drop until last night."

"Hmmm."

"You've got to admit there are certain advantages."

"I suppose so."

"You see any disadvantages?"

"Well...Look, Shar, we've all worked hard to build this agency, especially you. Do you really want to see it absorbed into a huge corporate entity?"

"No, but really..."

"Don't tell me you're afraid of rejecting Hy's offer? Harming your marriage? He doesn't have that kind of ego."

"I know."

"But you have reservations, right?"

"Yes. Maybe it's that as I get older I don't want to make changes or take risks."

He hooted. "You?"

"Sounds stupid, doesn't it? Or maybe it's just…January." Rain had started to spatter the windowpanes again.

"Maybe. Don't rush into anything, that's all I have to say."

"I won't."

He changed the subject. "What's next on the Warrick case?"

"I'm heading out to corral some people who won't want to talk with me."

10:37 a.m.

Caro Warrick's parents again didn't answer their phone, but there was a new message on the machine in a woman's voice.

You've reached Betsy and Ben. We're off for two glorious weeks in Cabo, but we'll check frequently for your calls. Adios.

Not a very smart message because it was an open invitation to any caller who might be inclined to commit burglary.

The Warricks had left before anyone was able to notify them that their eldest daughter was dead. I wondered if they would have postponed their trip had they heard.

No sooner had I ended the call than Inspector Fast

phoned. I told him I had been hired by Caro Warrick and asked if it was okay with him if I continued the investigation for her publisher. As I'd expected, he had no problem with that, and we made an appointment to discuss the case that evening, since he was working a late shift.

The day before, Rob Warrick had given me a set of spare keys to Caro's apartment and signed a permission slip to allow me to visit the premises in case the landlord objected. I decided to see if there was anything revealing in Caro's former home.

11:50 a.m.

Caro's apartment smelled even mustier on this morning than it had on my previous visit. I left the door open—the rain had eased up, leaving the air warmish—and opened a couple of windows. Then I sat down on the sofa, closed my eyes, and tapped into the feeling of the place.

It's long been my opinion that, even after a person has vacated a given location, an aura of them and what they did there remains. It's mystical and New Agey and I wouldn't admit it to my clients or in court, but it works for me. And in my profession, you use any tool that's effective.

As my breathing grew deeper, my hearing became keener. Bird sounds in the backyard, the creaking of an old joist in the ceiling. A TV mumbling somewhere, muted traffic sounds. Someone bouncing a basketball on the next block. The smell of mildew and aromatic wax was stronger. Under it a scent—flowery perfume, old-fashioned. Another scent—cleanser from the kitchen. I licked my lips: they tasted dusty, like the air around me.

My skin was tingling now. I felt a sudden chill from the open door and windows, then a rush of heat. My own heat. It faded, and I kept my eyes closed and let the impressions flood over me.

Unhappiness, yes—that was to be expected—but it was leavened with hope. And something else. Fear—just a little, such as one might feel when embarking upon a new enterprise. And another emotion…It eluded me.

Something I hadn't experienced, perhaps?

I slumped farther back on the sofa. The emotion became stronger. Anxiety…something hidden…something that somebody might find out…

I opened my eyes, stood up, and started searching.

Caro's possessions were few and orderly. Neatly folded underwear, neatly hung clothing. Her bed was made with tight corners. The bathroom was sparkling clean and smelled of shampoo. There was a grocery list tacked to the refrigerator by a magnet: cereal, bananas, chicken, veggies. Only milk and eggs and condiments were inside. She'd been due for a shop. In a low drawer I found files: rent receipts, tax returns, a copy of her lease for the apartment.

What interested me was the lack of truly personal items: photographs, letters, mementoes. The past didn't exist here. Nor did the future except in the presence of the will. And the feeling of hope.

I closed the windows, made sure the door was locked, and went to talk with the landlord.

12:47 p.m.

Mrs. Cleary must have been nearly eighty, with wispy white hair and deep vertical facial wrinkles. She hadn't been informed of her tenant's death and when I told her, her smile crumpled and her eyes sheened with tears.

"That poor girl," she said, clasping her heavily veined hands to her breasts. "She had such a tragic life."

"When was the last time you saw her?"

"Two or three days ago. I can't remember exactly. She was taking her mail from the box that's attached to the side of the garage."

"How did she seem?"

"Her voice was pleasant as always. I don't see so well any more, and the sun was in my eyes, so I'm not sure how she looked. But she sounded fine. After that I heard her—or someone—downstairs."

"Or someone?"

"Well, Caro's step was light, quick. A couple of times I heard a heavier tread."

"Could it have been mine?"

She squinted at me. "No, you're too slender. The footsteps I heard must have been a man's."

"What time was this?"

"In the evening. Before ten; I go to bed at ten."

"Can you narrow down the time frame?"

She frowned. "My granddaughter had called. She always calls at eight to check up on me. We didn't talk for long; nothing notable had happened to either of us. So maybe I heard the footsteps at a quarter past eight."

"Is there anything else you can tell me about Caro's last days?"

She thought, shook her head. "Nothing. She came and went so quietly—and now she'll never come home again."

1:10 p.m.

Since it was midday on a Friday, it seemed a poor time to canvass Caro's neighbors, but I decided to give it a try anyhow. I had a quick sandwich at a nearby deli and then went up and down both sides of her block, talking with those who were home. None of them had known of her death, and all expressed sorrow. Caro had not been close to them, but they knew her story and sympathized with her.

"She brought me some homemade apple butter just last October," a chubby, balding fellow said.

"She babysat for my kids once in a while," a young mother told me. "I wasn't afraid to leave them with her; I knew she was innocent. And they loved her."

"Why would anybody want to kill her?" an older man who was mowing his minuscule patch of front lawn asked. "She'd had more than her share of sorrow and still was as kind a woman as you'd ever hope to meet."

"Old lady Cleary kept the house dark on trick-or-treat night, but the kids knew to take the path to Caro's door. She always gave Hershey's Kisses."

"She shopped for my groceries once, when I was too sick to go to the store."

"She always brought Mrs. Cleary's garbage cans in, as well as her own."

Saint Caro? Or Caro the atoner? Or something in between?

3:36 p.m.

In spite of the sandwich I'd had, I was hungry, so I stopped
at home for a bite to eat. There was a note on the kitchen
table from Hy: "Gone to LA on company business. Call
you later."

Routine business? Dangerous? How the hell was I supposed to know? I thought again of his proposed merger
with my agency; if the business entities were joined, I
would insist on knowing the details of his activities, as he
would the details of mine.

I went to the fridge. Alex joined me and stood on his
hind legs, peering inside. The bottomless-pit cat. I settled
on ham and cheese on crackers; he joined me. I was spoil-
ing him, but I'd always spoiled my cats. Jessie appeared,
and I spoiled her too.

While we ate I considered my next move and decided
I might as well check with what neighbors of mine
I knew would be home, to ask if any of them had
seen Caro arrive here last night. The police would already have done this, but I thought maybe they'd missed
someone or someone would have remembered something they'd forgotten or hadn't wanted to reveal to
officialdom.

4:04 p.m.

Mrs. Irene Hall, next door to the right, gaunt, stooped, and all angles: "We went to bed early, honey. And our bedroom's at the back of the house like yours. We didn't hear a thing till the police came. Lord, as we grow older we just sleep sounder. Getting prepared, I guess."

At the Curley house to the other side of mine, daughter Michelle popped out. "Damn," she said, "I missed all the commotion. I was sleeping over at that place I'm rehabbing on Webster."

Chelle was a budding entrepreneur, having already refurbished a decaying cottage nearby and turned it for a profit.

I said, "Is that wise, sleeping alone in a half-derelict building?"

She rolled her eyes. "Shar, d'you think I was *alone*?"

Chelle was growing up, just like Jamie. I'd have to remember that.

"Were your folks home? Or Gwen?" Gwen Verke, Michelle's foster sister.

"Nope. Gwen was staying at a friend's from school, and my parents took a few vacation days and went to visit relatives in the Santa Barbara area—where it's not raining."

I felt a stab of envy for anyone who was anyplace where it wasn't raining. While growing up in San Diego I'd mistakenly assumed that mostly sunny, warm days were the norm. Even in Berkeley and San Francisco conditions were usually good. But then came global warming— which many people claim doesn't exist, but if not, how do you explain the polar ice melt and radical changes in weather patterns throughout the world? And the devastating flooding, tornadoes, hurricanes, and earthquakes in places where such disasters have never been heard of?

"You working a case?" Chelle asked. "Can I help?"

She'd helped me before; her parents would kill me if I enlisted her again.

"I've got this one under control," I said, "but if I need assistance, I'll call on you."

7:00 p.m.

Devlin Fast was punctual to the minute. He ushered me into his cubicle at exactly seven o'clock.

Fast was one of the department's black recruits who had risen quickly through the ranks in a period when the city was demanding racial diversity—in a way very similar to my operative Adah Joslyn, who had become their poster officer because she was female, half black, and half Jewish. Adah had gotten fed up with the bullshit of a police force in chaos and quit to work for me, but Fast was loyal and by-the-book. If he had his problems with the department—which I was sure he did, because he was an extremely intelligent man—he kept them to himself.

"So," he said as we sat across the desk from one another, "the Carolyn Warrick murder. She was your client?"

"Yes. She wanted me to reaffirm her acquittal, turn up more facts for a true-crime book she was coauthoring. What about the physical evidence in her murder—the hammer, blood?"

"The hammer was one you can buy in any Ace Hardware. Had been used, had some scoring on the head and claws, but not much. Prints on the handle belong to Ms. Warrick."

"So she might've brought it along with her as a defensive weapon. She never said anything to me, but she could have been afraid someone was following her."

"Paranoid, was she?"

"Could have been. I don't know—we only met twice, once in my office and once at her apartment."

"And you have no idea why she went to your house that night?"

"Yes, I do. She had an envelope with my name on it."

"The contents?"

"Old clippings about her case. Nothing I didn't already know. Probably the same as her biographer has."

"So why take them to you?"

"She wanted me to be current on how the project was going." God, the lies I tell! Must've learned that art when my parents made me go to confession.

I couldn't tell whether Fast believed me or not. He simply said, "Make me copies, will you?"

"Sure."

"You know, she'd hired a couple of PIs before. But unlike the other investigators she dealt with, you've got a reputation for results."

"May I have the names of the other investigators?"

"I'll e-mail them to you as soon as I've gone over the old files." He frowned. "I don't understand why Warrick would want to stir up trouble. My former partner was on the case, and I attended a couple of days of the trial. So let's say I'm dubious about the verdict."

"Please, give me your impressions."

Fast's broad face became contemplative. "Ms. Warrick was an obsessive personality, so much so that she turned down an offer to return to her former position at the SF Violence Prevention Center in order to undertake this...nonsensical pursuit. As for the facts of the case, a number of times she warned her ex-boyfriend Jake Green to stay away from Amelia Bettencourt. Green interpreted the warnings as threats. The evidence in the case was tampered with while in our custody."

"Which evidence?"

"The documents showing she had been licensed to own a Glock 19 had been expunged from the state records."

"Who could have done that?"

"Well, that's a good question. The dealer—Ralph Levinson here in the city—had a record of the sale and application for registration on file, but Sacramento had nothing."

"Maybe the application was never filed."

"Levinson says otherwise. Of course, he could be lying."

"Why would he?"

Fast shrugged. "He didn't file the papers and didn't want to be caught out as negligent. Or someone paid him to."

"Who?"

"The case involved people in high places. Your guess is as good as mine."

"I've spoken with Caro's brother and sister; they're in touch with her, but her parents are not."

"Those parents are one cold couple. Although they were defense witnesses, their testimony on the stand was almost hostile. Could be they thought she was guilty, but were doing whatever they felt parents should do—badly.

From their testimony it was apparent that they cared more for Amelia Bettencourt than their own daughter. I'll be interested to see how they behave now that she's dead."

"They're in Cabo San Lucas. I don't know if anyone's contacted them, but I wouldn't count on it. They didn't leave a number, and the surviving daughter and son seem indifferent to them."

"Lovely family." Fast's eyes became shadowed. "You know, I had a family once. Wife Cynthia and daughter Diane. It was smashed to hell when Diane died of a drug overdose and Cynthia left me. She couldn't live with a cop who wouldn't acknowledge that his own daughter was in trouble and take steps to prevent it. If I were the Warrick father, I'd be holding the rest of my family close right now."

I thought of my big extended family: those related by blood, by adoption, and by friendship. Although many of us were separated by long distances, I held them close every day of my life.

8:57 p.m.

I put in an hour at the office, finishing up the loose ends of my day. Then, mindful of Ted's admonishment, I ate a big seafood salad at Palomino, a favorite restaurant on the Embarcadero, across from shabby, doomed Pier 24½. Seeing the pier darkened and deserted made me nostalgic; the name of the restaurant made me think of Sidekick, Hy's Palomino horse stabled on our ranch in the high desert. And that made me miss King, my roan horse. I'd always hated horses until, on one fateful visit, King and I had bonded. I hadn't known what I'd been missing.

The salad and a glass of chardonnay energized me. I didn't want to go home just yet. The winter darkness when I came out of the restaurant made me think: what was Caro Warrick's apartment like after dark?

Places are different at night: Some things that stand out during the day are softened or erased entirely. Others become palpable, crying out for notice. When I bought my house here in the city, I insisted on seeing it before and after nightfall. It was the dark viewing that cinched the deal—the place had been and still was enveloping, not remotely threatening.

I headed for the Outer Sunset.

The light from the upper part of the house—Mrs. Cleary's—bathed the pathway to the garage apartment. When I got out of my car, I thought I saw a figure standing in the shadow of a yew tree next door. I took several seconds locking the car, pretending to fumble with the keys, while I acclimated to my surroundings. Something definitely felt wrong. I turned, putting my hands up to my eyes as I would a camera and pretending to search for an address. Nothing. The person was gone, or maybe had never been there—a figment of my overactive imagination.

Still the sense of wrongness persisted.

I went along the walkway toward the garage apartment. Wind rattled the leaves of the ivy on the fence, promising a colder turn to the weather. Over the rustling I heard what sounded like a footstep and looked back. No one in sight. Probably just someone walking by, but still I hesitated. Slipped back along the walkway and peered out at the street.

Empty.

Too many nighttime confrontations had made me wary of things that go bump after dark. When you've been shot in the head and almost died...

I used the keys Caro's brother Rob had given me, eased the door open and shut. A clock, which I hadn't noticed before, ticked softly. The refrigerator hummed. I could hear the beat of my pulse, slow and steady.

Again I felt the sense of loneliness, unhappiness, and faint hope that I'd had before. I switched on a table lamp and went prowling, turning on other lamps as I went. New details struck me: a crack in a cut-glass vase; a faint stain that looked as if it might've once been orange on the wall next to the sofa; a loose section of baseboard...

No, McCone. The baseboard's too obvious a hiding place, as obvious as the toilet tank.

Right. But I examined it anyway. The baseboard concealed nothing, looked as if it had been bashed by an overzealous person wielding a vacuum cleaner.

Nothing unusual here. Nothing that you wouldn't expect to find in a lonely single person's apartment.

But I still felt something was missing.

I locked up the apartment and went down the walkway. As I turned onto the sidewalk I spotted a dark figure, approximately the same size and shape as the one I thought I'd seen before, across the street. Abruptly the person turned and fled down an alley between two houses.

So I hadn't been imagining things before. Somebody watching Mrs. Cleary's house, perhaps with the idea of breaking in and finding something in Caro's apartment? Somebody following me? Or maybe just your garden-variety Peeping Tom? In any case, he—I assumed he was male because of his size—had a good head start on me. It would be foolish to go chasing him in that dark, unfamiliar territory.

10:14 p.m.

The blue building on Sly Lane was dark and deserted, only security lights winking in the underground garage to show me the way to the elevator. For a moment I paused before getting out of my car, remembering my earlier edginess at Caro's apartment and the night I'd been assaulted and shot at Pier 24½. Then I put the thoughts behind me: horrifying as many of my recollections were, I'd long ago made up my mind not to dwell on the past. I waited for the old, clanking elevator cage to reach garage level, then hit the button for the—grandly labeled—penthouse suite.

My office was cold. I turned up the thermostat, took the envelope of Xeroxed clippings from Caro Warrick from my bag, and retreated to my comfortable armchair. I reread the clips carefully, scanning for any detail I hadn't noticed before. The timeline was the same, as was the cast of characters. Even though only three years had passed, the paper felt brittle, was browning. The events reported might have occurred decades in the past.

But there was an article from last December that I had somehow skimmed or overlooked the night Caro was attacked. One of those end-of-the-year where-are-they-now pieces that newspapers sometimes run about sensational crimes.

Carolyn Warrick, of course, was still living and working in the city then.

Elizabeth and Benjamin Warrick resided in Millbrae. That I knew.

Amelia Bettencourt's mother, Iris, had died of a stroke the preceding August.

Bettencourt's father, James, had served two years' probation for assault with a deadly weapon and was currently living on the Monterey Peninsula.

Interesting. ADW is one of those crimes that lawyers call a "wobbler"—meaning it can be classified either as a misdemeanor or as a felony, depending upon various circumstances. The fact that James Bettencourt had received only two years' probation indicated that the DA hadn't considered the assault that Bettencourt had perpetrated too serious.

Jake Green lived in Atherton, an upscale suburb on the Peninsula. That gave me pause: Green had presented himself as down on his luck, ruined by the scandal following Amelia's murder. Of course, he could've bought the house before that, when he was making big money as a stockbroker.

Dave Walden, a close friend of both Amelia and Caro who had testified as a character witness for the defense, owned a winery up north in the Alexander Valley, with his wife, Kayla. I scanned through the clippings again; there was no other mention of Dave or Kayla Walden.

I turned to the computer to Google them. A few sounds

made me pause—metal on metal. I glanced at the old elevator to see if someone might be coming up, but the arrow on its dial remained at P.

Penthouse, my ass.

The problem, I thought, was that I didn't really like the building—or Sly Lane. I'd allowed Ted to talk me into leasing it because it was in proximity to the Embarcadero (and his apartment, now that I thought of it). He loved the place—especially its blue color, and the fact that it was a former whorehouse where the madam had been murdered in 1894.

But I felt isolated here on the hill, even though I wasn't very far away from the liveliness I had enjoyed on the Embarcadero: the salt tang in the air, the Bay breezes, the walkers and runners and bicyclers and roller skaters, the restaurants.

South of Market—SoMa—had changed since I'd moved the agency to Pier 24½, for the better and also for the worse. Construction was at an all-time high, with the resultant noise and dust, but many of the more ambitious projects had been halted by lack of funding. Many buildings that had sat empty because of the recession were now attracting tenants, and interesting new shops and restaurants abounded. The Museum of Modern Art had prospered and was soon to be expanded, and "parklets"— large boxes filled with ferns and other low-maintenance plants—brightened alleyways that I used to cut through on my way to and from the locations I frequented.

The good and the bad, I'd take all of it. But not this building. The blue façade looked downright frivolous. The clanking elevator cage annoyed or intimidated clients.

Having to run up and down stairs to have a face-to-face with staff members wasted time. But we'd signed a long-term lease.

I turned my attention back to Google. Walden Vineyards was located on Alexander Valley Road near Healdsburg, a prime wine-grape-growing area. The winery was small, producing only a few hundred cases of sauvignon blanc and zinfandel per bottling, and had been in operation seven years. The photos on the website showed a small, high-ceilinged tasting room and a terrace overlooking vine-covered hills topped with tall pines.

Tomorrow was Saturday; a jaunt to the valley could be pleasurable—and fruitful, in more ways than one.

I put my computer to sleep and pushed back from the desk. The arrow on the elevator still pointed to the "penthouse." For a moment I considered taking the stairs, then shrugged and pressed the button. The grille groaned and wheezed back, and I stepped on and pressed the Down button.

The elevator started, then stopped. I punched the button again. The elevator moved a few inches, then lurched violently to the right. I was thrown off balance, my shoulder slamming into the wall. Sparks of pain shot up my neck and down my arm.

What the hell...?

I clung to the handrail for a few seconds, my blood pounding in my ears. When I righted myself, the elevator floor groaned under me. Quickly I balanced my weight evenly in the middle.

Those noises I'd heard earlier—they weren't normal for an elevator at rest, but I'd been so involved with my searches that I'd dismissed them. Had somebody disabled it? Was that person still around?

I held on to the handrail and shifted my weight slightly. The cage stayed where it was.

I tried punching the buttons again, all of them. Nothing. Stuck.

There should have been an escape hatch on top of the cage through which I could climb, but when I looked up I didn't see one. Nor was there a phone I could use to call for help—not that it would've done any good, seeing as the building was deserted.

A small groaning noise.

If the car fell, would it go all the way to the underground garage, crashing on the hard concrete? How far was that? How much of an impact? Enough to seriously injure or even kill me.

My breath felt hot and constricted in my throat and chest. My lips and hands began tingling. Little pinpoints of light flashed in my eyes. I couldn't hyperventilate now!

Breathe slowly, shallowly. Don't suck air in through your mouth. In, out. In, out.

Finally the symptoms subsided, but the breathing exercise hadn't calmed me at all. I cursed the elevator, then the building, and then Sly Lane. When I got to Ted, I stopped. My fault. I should've looked into his recommendation of new quarters for the agency more thoroughly. But I'd been busy with a personal case and…

This isn't getting you out of here.

After a few minutes, I shifted my weight experimentally. There was a screech of metal on metal. The cage dropped about six inches, then stopped with a clunk. My hand slipped on the railing and I fell against the back wall. And then the lights went out.

I reached for the railing and pulled myself up an inch at a time to prevent any sudden motion from dislodging the cage. Once on my feet I held my breath and stood still. A slight creak, that was all.

Gingerly I took out my cell phone and speed-dialed Ted. Only his machine answered. I yelled into it in case he was screening his calls, but he wasn't. His cell didn't answer, either. Who else could help me?

The management company, of course. But I didn't have its number in this phone's address book, and its office wouldn't be open this late on a Friday night anyway.

Well, there was always 911.

Yeah, sure. Given emergency services' dismally long response time and the fact that they'd consider this a low-priority emergency, I'd probably be trapped here all night. Or worse, my continued weight would cause what must be frayed cables to break, the cage to fall. And if the media caught wind of my predicament…I could picture the humorous squib in the *Chron*: "Private Eye Can't Find Way Out of Own Elevator."

Call Hank.

Of course. Hank Zahn, my best friend from college, the agency's and my personal attorney. In all those years he'd never let me down, nor I him.

His line had buzzed once when the cage gave another lurch, throwing me to the floor. The phone, jarred loose, banged against one of the walls. I covered my head with my hands.

"Hello," Hank's voice said dimly.

I reached for the phone; it was too far away, and I didn't want to make a move that would send the elevator plunging to garage level.

"Hank," I yelled.

Silence.

"Help! Elevator on Sly Lane."

The cage jolted again, and I braced for the crash, but it stayed in place.

Had Hank heard me? Or had the cell connection been dropped? How long would that damnable thing hang there?

Sabotage, there was no doubt in my mind: the sound that had startled me earlier as I sat at my computer; the person I'd sensed watching me in Caro's neighborhood.

Why? My case was no threat to anyone—

A minor settling, and the cage tilted slightly to the right.

To avoid another attack of hyperventilation, I took small, short breaths, but the air in the cage had gotten stuffy, and my head felt light. Where was Hank? The call must've been dropped.

Another lurch, more screeching. I curled myself into a ball, arms protecting my head.

And felt the cage plummet down...

11:59 p.m.

"How many fingers am I holding up?"

"Two." I'd been down this route before.

"What day is it?"

"Friday, maybe Saturday by now."

"Your name?"

I tried to sit up. "I know my own name, dammit!"

Gentle but forceful hands pressed me back. "Your name, ma'am?"

"Sharon McCone, okay? 'Ms.', not 'ma'am.'"

A familiar voice from above my head said, "She's as belligerent as usual." Hank's face appeared. "Lie still and do what the paramedics tell you. You're not injured, just shaken up."

"Where did I end up? On the elevator, I mean."

"Conveniently, the first floor. You passed out. The elevator's shot."

"Good. I hate the goddamn thing! I hate this building! I hate—"

"Calm down. They'll be taking you to SF General to see if you have a concussion."

"No."

"Yes. Necessary precaution. You'll be released in the morning. I'll drive you home."

"No more hospitals!"

"Sssh." He laid a cool hand on my forehead. "I know how you feel, but it's best to let them check you out. I'll be right there with you. Is Hy in town?"

I shook my head; it hurt, but not much. "I don't want to bother him with this."

"But he's reachable?"

"Through RI's LA office. But don't—"

"I won't—yet."

I reached up and grasped his wrist. Our years together flashed through my mind: Sitting on the stairs at parties in the house a bunch of us had shared in Berkeley, pleasantly stoned on dope and idealism. Playing poker around the big oak table in All Souls' kitchen at the co-op's Victorian on Bernal Heights. The time he'd been shot and I'd been so terribly afraid he would die. His wedding to Anne-Marie Altman. Their party celebrating the adoption of their daughter Habiba Hamid. Good memories, bad ones—years of them.

"They're ready to transport you now," he said.

I gripped his wrist tighter.

"That's okay," he told me, peeling my fingers away. "I said I'd come with."

SATURDAY, JANUARY 7

11:30 a.m.

Hank helped me up my front steps and into my house as if I were an infirm old lady. The cats came running, then stopped, sensing something wrong.

"I'm a little battered, that's all," I told them.

"You still do that," Hank said.

"Do what?"

"Talk to cats."

"Most of the time they're better listeners than people."

He got me situated on the sofa, pulled the blue blanket around me. Fussed about placing one of the decorative pillows behind my head. "I'll make you some tea."

"You know I don't drink tea."

"Sorry, I forgot. Nearly everybody else I know grabs for the teapot when they're under stress. Coffee's your thing."

"Actually I'd rather have a drink."

"Shar, are you sure that's a good—"

The exasperation that I'd been holding in check boiled over. "Stop acting like a mother hen. Wine, I said. There's an open bottle of chardonnay in the fridge. A *big* glass of it, please."

He shot me a dubious look and went into the kitchen.

I leaned my head back, savoring the feeling of home. The cats came up on the sofa and sniffed at me, then hopped off. Hospital smells were not among their favorites. Hank returned with my wine—his definition of big gave it a whole new meaning. This glass would tide me over until midnight.

I sipped some of it.

"That stuff'll put you to sleep."

"I hope so."

"You planning to call Hy?"

"In a while."

"You know he'll go ballistic and rush up here."

"That's why I'm putting it off." I paused. "Hank, I *hate* that building on Sly Lane. The elevator's off-putting to the clients—and certainly now to me. I'm tired of running down stairs every time I want to speak personally to somebody. The parking situation's okay, but that's about it. I'll get Ted started on finding other quarters, and then you'll break the lease. We've plenty of grounds."

He nodded. "One phone call from me should do it. But what I find strange is that the elevator was inspected a few months before you took possession."

"It was tampered with."

"Possibly."

"No, more than possibly." I told him about the man I'd seen near Caro's apartment, the sounds I'd heard.

"But why?" he asked.

"Maybe whoever killed her thought she'd given me some information that would lead to them. All the more reason to get my staff out of there right away."

Hank sat next to me, patting my hand. "When you find a new place, I'll oversee the move."

"You don't have to do that."

"How many things have you done for me that you really didn't have to?"

"Friends." I sighed.

"Yeah, friends."

We sat silently for a moment. I sipped wine. Thought, *Good God, how did this huge glass get half empty?* After a while Hank went to replenish it, and when he came back I thought to ask after his adopted daughter, Habiba Hamid.

"She's great," he told me. "All A's in school, and into sports like kickboxing and karate. When she starts dating, I'll never have to worry about her taking shit off of any boy."

I smiled, remembering the frightened little girl I'd rescued off a remote Caribbean island a few years ago.

"Which one of you does she live with most of the time?" Hank and his wife, Anne-Marie Altman, had an interesting living arrangement: he was what he liked to call a "casual housekeeper"; she was what she admitted to being a "fascist homemaker." Once this had posed a problem, but now they owned a building with two flats, and each lived in a different one—with ample visiting privileges. Habiba alternated, depending on her mood.

Hank said, "She's into neat these days. Anne-Marie's teaching her to weave. But the kid's getting bored with it, so I suspect I'll be seeing more of her soon."

"What a great life she has." Was that my voice, slurring the words? "I've been meaning to ask you about her birthday…" I smiled again and put my head against his chest. "Dammit, Zahn, you drugged me."

"No, you drugged yourself with a little help from me. You could do with a few hours of sleep."

6:20 p.m.

"I'm coming back up there *inmediatamente*."

I smiled. Hy fluently spoke three languages besides English—Spanish, German, and Russian—and sometimes lapsed into one or another, depending upon which he'd recently been using. I assumed he'd been dealing with Hispanics over the course of the day.

"There's no need for that," I said. "But I want to ask you a question: that extra office space you have? Could the agency move into it until we find other quarters?" RI had purchased a small office building south of Market on Fremont Street when Hy moved its world headquarters north from La Jolla.

"Of course. You can move into it permanently; you know how I feel."

"Thanks. I'll keep the option open. Right now all I care about is protecting my staff. Tomorrow I'll ask as many of them as are available to go over to Sly Lane and collect computers and whatever else they need. I assume they can get access, since RI is a twenty-four-hour operation."

"I'll tell my people to expect them. Where will you be?"

"Off to the Wine Country."

SUNDAY, JANUARY 8

11:10 a.m.

The Alexander Valley, northeast of the quaint town of Healdsburg, is beautiful countryside: vineyards, old stone wineries, aggressively modern wineries, low oak-and-madrone-covered hills, and higher hills covered with pines. On a good day it's a delight. Unfortunately on this rainy Sunday in January it was gray and depressing.

For my purposes the gloom was perfect. There was little traffic on the two-lane highway, and there'd be few visitors at the tasting rooms. I drove slowly, squinting through the rain-spattered windshield, until I saw the sign for Walden Vineyards. It showed a peaceful pond, buildings misty in the background. As I drove along the graveled driveway, the actual pond materialized.

Walden Vineyards, Walden Pond. Had this pond been there initially, or had it been created for bucolic effect?

The winery itself was one of the splashy, modern sort—lots of wood and tile and clerestory windows and skylights. I parked beside the only vehicle in the lot—a mud-splattered blue pickup truck.

Inside, light gleamed down on a terrazzo floor from dozens of tiny spots mounted on the high beams of the ceiling. A copper-covered bar fronted a wall of wine racks. The customary souvenirs and gift items with winery logos—T-shirts, openers, fancy corks, glasses, cookbooks—were displayed on tables around the perimeter. Above them the walls were hung with landscapes and abstract paintings, all for sale. Local artists, I thought. Some quite good and all with a hefty price tag, I suspected.

A raven-haired woman behind the bar looked up as I came in. She was wearing a stunning purple-and-gold cape that swirled around her slender body.

"Our first visitor today!" she exclaimed. "I was getting downright lonesome here. Are you planning to taste?"

"Sounds good," I told her and consulted their wine list. "Chardonnay, please." I watched while she expertly uncorked a bottle, poured a dollop into an oversized glass, and recited the usual spiel: "Sand Hill Chardonnay 2000, from the vineyards directly behind the winery. Light but not sweet, with a hint of grapefruit."

Before I tasted it, I set my credentials on the counter.

She studied them and her eyebrows rose. Then she extended her hand. "Kayla Walden, co-owner. I've never met a private investigator before. I assume you're here for something other than wine."

I sipped the chardonnay. Damned if I couldn't taste the grapefruit.

I complimented her on the wine and her cape.

"I collect capes, all kinds. They hide an infinite number of body flaws. But you're not here to talk about fashion."

"No. You're acquainted with a woman named Carolyn Warrick?" I asked.

Her gaze shifted, just a fraction. "No. Should I be?"

"Your name—and your husband's—was mentioned in a newspaper article about her." I took a copy of the clipping from my bag and indicated the part that I'd earlier high-lighted.

After a moment she said, "Well, they got the part about us owning the winery right. But I don't recall—"

A door behind the bar opened and a tall man came through carrying a case of wine. "More of the oh-eight zin," he said. "Not that we'll need it on such a dismal day."

"My husband, Dave," Kayla Walden said to me. "Dave, this is Sharon McCone, a private investigator from the city. Our names are mentioned in this newspaper article, but I've never heard of the woman or the case."

Dave Walden set down the wine and took the sheet from her hand. After scanning it, he handed it back to me and said, "Beats me. Dave Walden's a common enough name. Maybe they got their facts wrong."

A subtle tension was building between the two of them now. They didn't look at each other, and their body lan-guage had changed. I stuffed the paper into my bag, fin-ished the wine in my glass. "Probably. I understand you make outstanding zins."

"Coming right up," Dave Walden said—too heartily. "But since you like chardonnay, try our Estate Reserve first."

11:50 a.m.

I spent another twenty minutes at the winery, chatting up the Waldens. They were both personable and forthcoming about the winemaking process. When I asked, "Where do you source your fruit?"—an insider's expression that I'd picked up from a friend who worked the tasting bar at Monticello in the Napa Valley—they told me the grapes came from Hewette Vineyards, a little to the west on the highway. But every time I steered the conversation to my surprise at the *Chron*'s erroneous mention of them in connection with the Warrick trial, they insisted the facts must have been skewed and turned to other topics. They had me half believing them—but only half—when I left.

At the end of the driveway I noticed a delivery tube for the SF *Chronicle*. If the Waldens read it—and you could be sure they would, given the high price for delivery this far from the city—they would've seen the where-are-they-now piece. I'd suspected as much: their innocent glaze had been flawed.

I paused there for an oncoming string of cars, thinking over our conversation. When traffic cleared, I turned west toward Hewette Vineyards.

12:05 p.m.

Russ Hewette was a sharp-eyed man with a shock of white hair, probably in his seventies. His redwood home sprawled over a hillside above the terraced vineyards.

When I told him I was a friend of the Waldens, he led me into one of those modular, glass-covered rooms that people add onto their houses when they run out of space, where he insisted on serving me a glass of Walden Zinfandel 2001.

"Those're great kids," he said, gesturing toward the Walden winery. "I've known them since they bought the old Godden place, six, maybe seven years ago. All the Goddens are gone now, unless you count Jethro Weatherford, a shirttail cousin who lives on a quarter acre that was deeded to him by Gene Godden some twenty years ago."

"Where is that quarter acre?"

"Down the highway a ways, in a grove of gum trees. Worthless land, but Jethro seems happy there. He's kind of simple, has a drinking problem, hangs out at the Jimtown Store. They tolerate him, I think, because he's local color."

"About the Waldens—they've been here seven years?"

"Well, sure. But they're your friends; you ought to know that."

"We've been out of touch, and this was a short visit, so we didn't get to catch up completely."

"From the city, aren't you?"

"Yes."

"Don't go there much any more. It's changed, parking's terrible, and now they're putting in those new meters that you've got to be a genius to operate. You like it there?"

"Yes, yes I do." In spite of its numerous faults, San Francisco was home.

"Well, you're young. The city's for the young or the rich. Or the flat-out poor." He held his glass up to the light, admiring the wine's color. "So why did Dave and Kayla ask you to drop in on me?"

I'd already manufactured a reply to that particular question. "My husband and I are considering buying property up this way. I'm talking to a lot of people in the area."

"Hope you're well fixed. Real-estate market is dead most places, but it's booming here."

"Dave and Kayla told me they'd gotten quite a deal—"

"That was years ago. Things change."

"Do you see them often?"

"Why, we talk on the phone every now and then."

A thought nudged at me; God knows where ideas come from. "When did you last actually see them, though?"

"Why? Something wrong over there?"

"Well, I'm not sure. Something was off, anyway—the reason I made it a short visit."

"I see Dave in the vineyards now and then, working with his crew."

"You don't deal with him directly on the grapes he buys from you?"

"No. His field manager handles that. Dave's strictly a winemaker."

"And Kayla?"

"Every morning she leaves fresh-baked bread on the porch, early before I'm out of bed. Always has."

"When did you last have a personal conversation with either of them?"

A long pause. "Two, maybe two and a half years ago. They're not very social people, keep pretty much to themselves."

They'd seemed social enough with *this* stranger in their tasting room. Why not with their neighbor?

3:37 p.m.

I sat at a small table inside the Jimtown Store, an old-fashioned Alexander Valley institution, eating a bowl of its Chain Gang Chili and sipping a glass of its Jimtown White. In good weather the store—filled with Wine Country antiques, local products, T-shirts, postcards, souvenirs, jars of candy and cookies—would be mobbed. But today, except for the counterman and a scruffy individual nursing a drink whose contents seemed to come from a bottle in the pocket of his raincoat, the place was deserted.

The scruffy man kept stealing glances at me. I glanced back, smiled encouragingly. Finally he got up and approached my table. Leaned on the extra chair. "You alone, miss?"

This had to be Jethro Weatherford, shirttail cousin of the Goddens. On the way into town I'd stopped at the grove of gum trees—another term for eucalyptus—that the former winery owners had deeded to him, but his small cabin had been locked and deserted.

I looked into his bleary eyes. Saw sadness and loneliness. "Yes, I'm alone. Would you care to join me?"

"Thank you, miss, I would." He extended a gnarled hand. "Jethro T. Weatherford."

"Sharon McCone."

With difficulty he lowered his frail, lanky body into the chair. "You're not from around here. Unless you're one of the new people."

"New people?"

"The ones who're coming up here, disturbing the balance of life. Everything's changing, and I hate change."

"You've lived here a long time."

"All my life. Was born on the old Godden place. My father was foreman there, my mother helped out in the house. They're gone, all of them now."

"The new people who own the winery—do you know them?"

He moved his hand in dismissal. "Nope, they're not friendly. In fact, I hear the woman's downright crazy. Was waving a gun around a few years back, threatening to kill herself. Fellow I know who works for them said the husband had to talk her down, give her a shot."

Whatever had been wrong with Kayla back then, the friendly, self-possessed woman I'd talked with in the tasting room had obviously overcome it.

Weatherford added, "A couple of years ago some lawyer came to see me. Asked if I would sell my place to them Waldens. Hell, no, I said, I'm too goddamn old to start over. He came back a few times, tried his damnedest to get me to sell. Finally he went away, and I never heard from him again."

"Do you remember his name?"

"Nope, but I've got his card somewheres. I kept it, just in case. I mean, what if I get disabled? Nice nursing homes are expensive, and I can't count on my no-good daughter

Nina to help out. Big career down in Hollywood, produces animated films. Not married, got no kids, but does she chip in to help her own father? No, she does not."

"Can you locate the lawyer's card for me?"

"Sure. It's in one of the kitchen drawers. Tell you what: I gotta get back home, feed and water my sheep. They wait for their treat—wheat and oats with honey—every day this time. You give me an hour, then come ahead. I'll have that lawyer's card for you."

I lingered at the table, enjoying a second glass of Jimtown White. After nearly fifty minutes had passed, I left the store and drove the short distance down the highway to Jethro Weatherford's property. The sheep were in an enclosure to the left side of the cabin, happily noshing on their food. There were deep tire gouges in the soft earth in front of the cabin, and I had to maneuver around them to keep the low-slung Z4's undercarriage from scraping.

Rain dripped from the eucalypti and their menthol-like smell was strong. I moved under them to the porch of the small structure. The screen door was closed, but the inner one stood open. I knocked on the frame and called out to Jethro.

No response.

A feeling of wrongness stole over me, and I knocked and called out louder. No sound from within.

I pulled the screen door open and stepped inside.

The old man was sprawled on the floor to the right, over the threshold of a living room. His white hair was soaked with blood; it had spread across the side of his face onto the pine floor. His skull was caved in.

My stomach lurched. Feeling a mixture of anger and sadness, I went to him, knelt, felt for a pulse.

Gone.

Who had done this? And why?

I looked around for the weapon that had killed him. A bloody brick lay on the floor just inside the living room. I rocked back on my heels, pictured the tire gouges in the mud outside: they had stopped in front of the cabin, made a sharp turn, and gone back toward the road. Wide tires on a heavy vehicle that sank deeply into the mud. A crime lab could get a good fix on what kind they were.

Jethro couldn't have been dead long; he'd had time to feed his sheep before he was attacked. He must have just walked into the house when his assailant hit him. The attorney's card was probably still in one of the kitchen drawers.

The kitchen was at the rear of the house—reasonably tidy, although the floor could have used a washing. My shoes stuck briefly to what were probably wine drippings in front of the refrigerator, and there was a tomato-red splotch in front of the sink. I began rummaging through the drawers: rubber bands, phone book, pens and pencils. Paper clips, empty eyeglass cases, miscellaneous and unidentifiable plastic parts. A hammer, bags of screws and nails. Checkbooks dating back to the early 2000s.

No lawyer's card.

But Jethro had seemed so sure it was in the kitchen.

Then I thought of the bag of cards that I'd bought last year in anticipation of several friends' and relatives' birthdays. I'd assumed I'd put them into the top drawer of my at-home filing cabinet, only to find them ten months later in the bottom drawer at the office. If I could make such a mistake at my age...

I began prowling through the rest of the house and found the card under some paperback books—spy novels—in the drawer of a prim little Victorian table in the living room. Gary Wells, with offices in Healdsburg. This was a homicide, and the investigators would need the lawyer's card. Quickly I snapped a photo of it with my cell, then called 911 and went outside to wait for the sheriff's deputies.

5:53 p.m.

The officers had arrived, the crime scene people had taken their photographs and collected their evidence. Jethro Weatherford's body was on its way to the morgue, and I was on my way home, still wondering if his sudden murder had anything to do with his conversation with me about my investigation.

He was such an innocuous old man, but drank too much and talked too freely to strangers. But there had been no sign that he'd been robbed, the only other motive I could think of, and it hadn't looked as if he'd had anything worth stealing anyway.

Before I left the Alexander Valley I called the number on the lawyer's card. Left a message, in case he checked his voice mail on Sundays. As soon as I disconnected, a call came in from Hy.

"McCone, where are you?"

"Novato."

"Are you okay?"

It seemed to me I'd heard that question hundreds of times—not only since I'd suffered from locked-in syndrome, but since I'd begun practicing my profession.

"I'm okay, okay, okay."

"Just wondering." He sounded wistful; we'd had so little time together of late.

"I'll be home within the hour."

The cell rang again. The lawyer, Gary Wells, returning my call.

I explained my reason for contacting him, and he said, "Yes, I remember Jethro Weatherford. A golfing buddy of mine, Dave Walden, asked me to contact him about selling his property."

"Why did your friend want it?"

"To complete his vineyard's acreage. Weatherford didn't want to sell, so that was that."

"Jethro Weatherford died this afternoon."

"I'm sorry to hear that. Of what?"

"He was murdered."

"What? By whom?"

"A person or persons unknown."

"Poor old man. What's to become of his land? I'm sure Dave would still like to have it."

Typical lawyer comment. Always thinking of a potential fee.

"That will depend on what Mr. Weatherford's heirs decide."

"Heirs? That hermit—"

"He has a daughter, Nina, who lives in Southern California."

A long pause. "Do you have her contact information?"

"I'm not at liberty to give that out," I lied, "but I'm sure you won't have any difficulty accessing it."

As I ended the call, I thought, *But you won't access it before I will.*

7:10 p.m.

Nina Weatherford said, "Oh my God, not Daddy."

"From something he said to me, I take it the two of you weren't close."

"…No, not really. We were until my mom died, but then I asked him to move down here, and he wouldn't. He wanted me to come home, but he didn't understand that Southern California is where I make my living. The last time we spoke, we quarreled about that; he said 'girls' didn't need to support themselves. Their 'upkeep' was supposed to be provided by their fathers or husbands."

"An old-fashioned gentleman; I sensed that."

"Old-fashioned, but always a gentleman." Nina Weatherford was crying now. After a moment she got herself under control and asked, "What's your connection with him?"

"I'm investigating a case involving some people who wanted to buy his land. I spoke with him at the Jimtown Store—"

"Daddy's hangout."

"Yes. He said he had an attorney's card that might've been of help to me, and went home to find it. When I arrived there he was dead."

"How was...?"

"A blow to the head."

"Did he suffer?"

"No. He died instantly."

"Oh, God, I should've *made* him move down here. Driven up and collected him and his damn stuff and dragged him to my house. I should've known it would come to this. I should've..."

"Should've known what, Ms. Weatherford?"

A long silence, and then Nina Weatherford broke the connection.

9:14 p.m.

Hy and I had no sooner finished dinner than he received a phone call from RI's Denver office requesting his presence in the morning.

"I'll call the pilot and ask him to preflight Six-Oh-Six right away," he told me. "It's a comfortable ride, I can sleep and be fresh for this new crisis by our eight o'clock meeting."

Six-Oh-Six: the Cessna Citation, an eight-seater, luxurious, and the fastest private jet so far manufactured, which RI kept at Oakland Airport.

I tried not to look disappointed, but he sensed my mood.

"After I get back, I'll take some time off and we'll fly up to the ranch or Touchstone."

"If *I* can take some time off."

"You know, if we merged our agencies, we could schedule more compatibly."

"There'd still be crises."

"Sure. That's what this business is all about."

After Hy threw some things into a flight bag and left, I sat in the parlor for a long time, pondering my resistance to change. If Hy and I merged our agencies, things would work out well, I knew that. So why did I want to cling to the old days, the old ways? It wasn't that I felt insecure; in many ways I'd never felt so secure in all my life. Secure in my marriage and Hy's love for me, secure in my profession, secure with my friends and family. It didn't make sense.

I got up and went to my home office, where I booted up my laptop. The cats joined me, staring greedily at the fish in the aquarium we'd recently purchased.

"Don't even think of it," I said.

They ignored me and licked their chops.

My earlier search on Walden Vineyards had been cursory, but now that I knew Dave Walden had been interested in buying Jethro Weatherford's small plot of land, I went deeper. I was interested to find out that the backing funds for the not-quite-profitable vineyards came from a trust that Kayla's late parents had set up for her. I didn't have the computer skills to get at the terms of the trust, but Mick did.

I called him at the Millennium Tower condo that he and Alison shared.

"It's Sunday night!" he exclaimed. "Are you nuts?"

"Probably."

"We're watching *The Wasp Woman!*"

Whatever that was. "Alison can DVR the rest of it for you."

The sound that he made was similar to what came out of Jessie when Alex was deviling her—half growl, half hiss. "So give me the details. I'll get back to you. And in exchange, I'm taking tomorrow morning off."

Now that was a gift: on Monday mornings Mick could make Ebenezer Scrooge seem cheerful.

11:35 p.m.

"The terms of the trust are these," Mick told me. "Kayla Walden—formerly Kayla Chase—is sole beneficiary of a sixty-five-million-dollar trust set up for her by her father, Anthony Chase."

"Anthony Chase—Chase Oil and other enterprises, right?"

"Right. Kayla was his only daughter, and her mother died of breast cancer in her late thirties. The trust places few stipulations upon her, except that if she predeceases her husband, he inherits a certain amount, but the winery and the capital revert to the trust, which in turn donates it to various breast cancer research organizations."

"Well, she looked healthy this afternoon. I liked her, her husband too."

"Then why're you—"

"It's got to do with their insistence that Dave had nothing to do with the Warrick case."

"The *Chron*'s not always right, you know."

"Do I ever! The things they've said about me...Still, here's your next assignment: contact the writer of the where-are-they-now piece and ask where her information came from. I'd ask you to contact the reporter who covered the trial—Jill Starkey—but I'm afraid she might do serious damage to sensitive parts of your anatomy. I'll tackle Starkey."

"Thanks. Nobody touches my junk except Alison. But are you gonna be okay?"

That question again!

"I've gone up against her before. This time I'll be carrying a big stick."

MONDAY, JANUARY 9

7:37 a.m.

I was finishing my second cup of coffee and contemplating my next approach to Jill Starkey when the phone rang and a man identified himself as Mr. Snelling, a representative of the management company for the building on Sly Lane.

"We're aware of the unfortunate situation with the elevator on Friday night," he said, "and would like to compensate you for your, ah, inconvenience. We could—"

"I'm not a litigious person, Mr. Snelling, although my firm's attorney will be in touch with you about terminating the lease, effective last Friday. Has anyone inspected the elevator?"

"We had a man out there yesterday."

"Was there evidence it had been tampered with?"

"Possibly. One of the cables was frayed, but it could've been overlooked by the earlier inspectors."

"Do you believe that?"

"Yes and no. The new man showed the cable to me, but I haven't the expertise to evaluate what happened."

I had no reason to doubt him; it was to his advantage to persuade me to return.

As I'd expected, he said, "Are you sure you won't reconsider and stay, Ms. McCone?"

"I'm very sure; we've already arranged for other quarters."

"In that case, we'll send you a check for the unused portion for the rent."

"That's very kind of you, Mr. Snelling."

"I'm not litigious either. Makes the world a better place."

Amen to that. At least he appeared to be conscientious and good at his job. I told him I needed to return to the building to make sure my staff had removed everything and that I would leave my keys, along with theirs, on the table in the foyer.

8:40 a.m.

Ted was the only one at the Sly Lane building when I arrived, and he was emptying the contents of his desk into a cardboard carton. He said, "The others are all getting settled into the new office suite. Pretty posh digs. Can we afford them?"

"They're sublet from RI. Hy cut me a deal."

"He still talking about a merger?"

"Off and on."

"And your thinking?"

I shrugged. "Let's see how it goes being next door to them before we make that decision."

"'We'?"

"Of course 'we.' All the employees of this agency have to be in accord on major issues."

"You weren't in accord about moving here, but you didn't express it. You hate this building."

"Well, it kind of charmed me at first. *Now* I hate it."

"Me too."

I handed him my keys. "Will you pick up everybody else's too, and leave them in the foyer?"

"Sure. I'll be back and forth all day. Not everybody could come in and move their stuff yesterday, and you can't believe the shit that's lying around unclaimed. Finicky Fags are coming at one o'clock to move the big stuff."

Finicky Fags—an only-in–San Francisco phenomenon—had been founded in the early 1990s by two gay teenagers just out of high school and without job prospects. In thirty-plus years it had grown to a firm with facilities throughout the state. While most of their employees and customers were gay or lesbian, a large number of heteros used their services. It was true that they were finicky: breakage or other damage seldom happened, and claims were promptly paid. Their storage facilities were reputed to be the best in the Bay Area.

I said, "Ted, you know one of the owners of Finicky Fags pretty well, don't you?"

"Neal does. They carted stuff around for his bookshop all the time."

"Do you think Neal could find out from him about self-storage facilities in south San Francisco?"

"*I* could do that by looking in the phone book."

"But if Neal's friend were to ask, he could probably

find out which one of them Caro Warrick rented a unit from."

"I gotcha. I'll ask Neal to get onto it right away. Where're you off to now?"

I glanced at my watch and sighed. "Unfortunately, to Caro Warrick's memorial service."

"They put that together quick. She only died on Thursday."

"There weren't a lot of people to invite, and the family didn't want the press to hear about it."

"Her parents coming back from Mexico for it?"

"As far as I know, the parents aren't even aware she's dead."

10:00 a.m.

I hate funerals and memorial services. At the former, with the body on display, people are supposed to confront and mourn a lifeless version that barely resembles the person they knew. I've noted that attendees tend to congregate at the opposite end of the room from the casket. Even with the casket closed, there is a haunting vision in one's mind of a friend or loved one made up to a mannequin's perfection by a mortician.

Memorial services these days are supposed to be touching and, in most cases, jovial. Family and friends are expected to tell humorous and inspirational tales about the dearly departed one's time on earth. Trouble is, even the funniest stories are tinged with sorrow, and many of the deceased didn't have particularly happy or significant existences.

I'd made Hy promise to toss my ashes off the cliff at Touchstone alone if I died first. He wanted the same.

One thing Caro's sister and brother knew was that she had wanted to be remembered in a favorite place: the Chinese Pavilion, on Strawberry Hill Island in Golden Gate Park's Stow Lake—a pagoda-style gift from our sister city, Taipei. The roof of the small round building is a pale green that contrasts with the darker shades of the surrounding trees, shrubs, and marsh grass; figures of mythical beasts appear to be scaling it; the support posts are bright red; on the slope above it looms the Strawberry Hill reservoir.

This morning was dry, and the sun was breaking through the fog, promising a warm day. The gathering was small: Rob, Patty, Mrs. Cleary, Ned Springer, and two colleagues from the real-estate agency where Caro had worked. No clergyman.

Rob coughed and said, "We're here to remember Patty's and my sister and your friend, Caro Warrick. Just Caro: when she was old enough to talk, two syllables were all she could master, and the nickname stuck. Caro had a difficult last few years, but her courage under adversity was an example to us all. We—"

He paused, looking off at the stone footbridge to the island. Everyone else's heads turned.

An attractive middle-aged couple wearing inappropriate casual clothing were crossing. The woman—blond, tanned, slim—raised a hand in greeting as if she were arriving at a party. Betsy and Ben Warrick, I thought, late for their eldest daughter's memorial.

I glanced back at Rob. He stood still, unsmiling, clenching his hands at his sides. Patty made a choking noise and said to Rob, "How could you let them know? They don't deserve to be here!"

"I left a message at their hotel. They had a right to know, but I never dreamed they'd come—"

Patty whirled around and pushed into the foliage beside her. Ned Springer made an I'll-take-care-of-her signal to me and followed.

Betsy Warrick went directly to Rob and threw her arms around him. "Oh, I'm so sorry, sweetie! So sorry."

He stood rigid, his face contorted with what I took to be revulsion.

Ben Warrick moved to stand beside them, his hand on Rob's shoulder. "We came as soon as we could, Son."

Rob threw off his father's hand, pushed his mother away from him.

"Fuck you! Fuck both of you! You made Caro's life hell, and now you won't even allow her a decent memorial by staying away!" He ran off the way Patty and Springer had gone.

Mrs. Cleary and the real-estate women were fleeing. Leaving me alone with the Warricks.

"And who are you, young lady?" Ben demanded. He, like his wife, was evenly tanned and slim, with blond, well-styled hair.

I was tempted to lie, say I was just an old colleague of Caro's, but the couple were so obnoxious that I decided to inject one more of what I was sure they would call "complications" into their lives. I took out my card and handed it to him.

He read it, his eyebrows rising. "Private investigator?"

"I'm assisting the San Francisco Police Department in their investigation into Caro's death. If you'd like confirmation, please call Homicide Inspector Devlin Fast at the Hall of Justice."

"But why—?"

"Because they're shorthanded, I'm very good at what I do, and Caro was my friend."

"Friend? My daughter had no friends after she murdered Amelia Bettencourt."

Something flickered in my memory: Inspector Fast, whose instincts I trusted, had told me the Warricks had seemed to be fonder of Amelia than of their own daughter. Then I looked at Betsy Warrick's eyes and revised the opinion: only Ben had been fonder of Caro's best friend.

I said, "I've intruded upon your grieving, so I'll be going now."

"No," Betsy Warrick said. "I want to hear more about Carolyn's last days. Please. Please have lunch with us."

11:50 a.m.

Lunch, of course, had to be at an expensive restaurant— Boulevard in the historic Audiffred Building near the Hyatt Embarcadero, where the Warricks were staying. I voiced no opposition to their choice: I love the place. And I didn't rein myself in, ordering my favorite starter—ahi tuna tartare—and main course—wood-roasted chicken breast with all sorts of wonderful ingredients. Ben Warrick selected an excellent chardonnay for me and his wife, and an equally good zinfandel for himself.

The talk around the table was somber: Why had Carolyn hired me? So she could confirm information for the book she and Greta Goldstein were writing. Did I know this Greta Goldstein? I'd only spoken with her on the phone, but she had an excellent reputation. Why had Carolyn needed this book to be published? She'd never felt she'd been completely exonerated of killing Amelia Bettencourt, and probably she'd needed the money.

Carolyn had never needed for money, Ben protested. She'd had an ample trust fund set up by her grandmother, and if more had been required, he and Betsy would have provided it.

Perhaps she'd felt the urge to be independent? I asked.

No, Betsy said, the trust provided her at least three thousand dollars a month.

So why, I wondered, was she living in a dreadful garage apartment and working at a low-paying job that she hated?

Well, there was the obvious—blackmail—but I didn't think that was the case. Self-castigation, maybe? Or did she donate most of her income to gun control causes?

"Did you speak to your daughter often?" I asked. "Write to her?"

"No, we did not."

"What about Rob and Patty?"

"We have…issues with them too. Obviously, as you saw at Stow Lake."

"Every family has its issues," I said, thinking of my own

far-flung and vastly different clans, "but in times of extreme trouble, most pull together."

Ben slapped his open hand onto the table so hard that Betsy looked alarmed.

"Do you have any idea," he said in a low but rage-filled voice, "what those children did to us? My son shot and killed his baby sister. My daughter slaughtered her best friend and got away with it. The other one, Patty, is a lesbian—a *vocal* lesbian. Turn on the TV news and there'll be Patty, fat and slovenly and yapping about gay rights."

"Ben...." Betsy put her hand on his arm. He shook it off.

"After that trial, my clients drifted away from me. Who's going to entrust their portfolios to a man with a freak show of a family? She"—he motioned to his wife—"is supporting us now. Most of her clients are women, and women are stupidly forgiving."

Betsy said, "Ben, stop—"

But he yanked her out of her chair and began dragging her toward the exit. I—and the other patrons—watched, stunned.

I was even more stunned when the waiter placed the bill on the table.

1:40 p.m.

By the time I got to our new offices in the RI building, I was so angry I felt as if great clouds of steam were billowing out of my ears. Not about getting stuck with the lunch check, but about the callousness the Warricks had displayed toward their children. Tragic accidents occur, people are unjustly accused, children often don't share the same definition of sexuality as their parents. But arrogance and hostility solve nothing. Nobody wins.

Kendra wasn't at her desk in the reception area, and fortunately Ted's door was closed. I didn't want to talk with anybody till I cooled down.

I hadn't seen the new suite, but I'd known what it would be like from frequent visits to RI's similar layout. Still, as I moved along the hallway, I was impressed. Pale gray walls, with luxurious medium-gray carpeting that would soothe the feet of the most harried of clients. Attractive, modern furnishings, designed for both comfort and function. Brightened by colorful posters or photographs, the décor would be stunning.

Even after all that, I wasn't prepared for my office at the end of the hallway: an expansive view from the Golden Gate to the Bay Bridge and East Bay hills; a long cherry-wood desk and workstation; floor-to-ceiling bookcases; clients' armchairs upholstered in a subtle gray-on-gray pattern. And best of all, my own leather armchair and hassock positioned by the window under a potted scheflera plant that spread its healthy leaves and branches in the early afternoon light.

The plant brought tears to my eyes. For years I'd had one in my office at All Souls, but when we'd moved to the pier it had taken a dislike to the place and died; its successor had had the same reaction to Sly Lane. I went over to the new one and fondled its trunk. "You and I are in this for the long haul, right?"

"Yeah, you are."

I started. Ted stood in the doorway, grinning.

"This"—I gestured around—"was all your doing, right?"

"Well, with the help of the interior decorator, yes."

"But this plant—"

"Whose name, by the way, is Mr. T."

"T as in Ted?"

"Right. Mr. T has a pedigree. Comes from a nursery Neal and I found up in Napa County. We have papers to prove it. In fact, Mr. T arrived by limo only fifteen minutes before you got here."

"A *limo*?"

Ted shrugged. "Actually, it was only a panel truck, but they have PLANT LIMO painted on its sides."

I went to him and threw my arms around his neck. "You are an amazing man," I said. "You've managed to turn one of the ugliest days of my year into the best."

He patted my back. "I hate to remind you, Shar, but it's only January."

2:31 p.m.

I tried to call Jill Starkey, at both her office and her home. No replies. Probably out gathering more dirt on more victims. Not necessarily innocent victims, but most of them people who didn't deserve her poisonous prose. Starkey was the sort of journalist who would continually twist facts for her own wicked enjoyment. Briefly I wondered what had made her that way.

Ted came into the office and with great ceremony slipped a note across the beautiful new cherrywood desk: his friend at Finicky Fags moving company had found that Caro Warrick had leased a self-storage unit from YouStor in south San Francisco. My first call from my elegant new quarters was to Rob Warrick.

"How're you doing?" I asked.

"Okay. I've managed to avoid the Parents from Hell. Patty's not so good; her therapist recommended a 'restful week' in a place where she's stayed before down near Santa Barbara."

"You think it'll help?"

"For a while anyway."

"Caro mentioned a self-storage unit in South City. Do you have a key to it?"

"No," he said, "but you do. It's on that ring of keys I gave you so you could get into her apartment."

I took them from my bag and located one that looked to be padlock-size; the tag attached to it said 1108.

"How do these places operate?"

"What do you mean?"

"Can you just drive in and go to your unit? Do you have to sign in or present identification?"

"Damned if I know. I suppose if I met you there, as holder of her power of attorney and executor of her estate, there'd be no problem."

"Do you have time to do that?"

"Plenty. The stock markets here are closed, and my clients in Asia are just waking up. Plus if there's a problem, I'm wired up to my teeth with Internet crap. I'll leave now, meet you there whenever traffic permits."

3:47 p.m.

As it turned out, there was no problem getting to Caro's storage unit; no one was on guard at the gate, so I drove in and meandered along the aisles till I found it. Rob wasn't there yet, so I parked and opened the door with the key on her ring. It must've been eighty degrees inside on this sunny afternoon, and I wondered how anything fragile could survive in that kind of heat.

The shed was full of boxes stacked against the side walls. The rear wall was taken up by a handsome cabinet—a modern Chippendale knockoff, I thought, and much too large for Caro's tiny apartment. Wiping sweat from my forehead, I started in on the cabinet; the boxes I could take outside and go through in the cooler air.

The drawers of the cabinet were filled with fine linen tablecloths and napkins; some looked hand-embroidered, all looked unused. A bunch of varicolored candles had melted into a blob. On a shelf to one side were some pieces of expensive-looking china—not enough to make a set—and a chest full of sterling silver in an excessively ornate pattern.

The linens, I thought, were the sort of thing often given to young women who were expected to make a good marriage. The same for the china and silver. But Caro had always lived in small places after she left the family home. What use did she have for such a large cabinet? Again, it had probably been given to her in expectation of her future life, a life that had failed to materialize.

I went through the boxes carefully, dragging them out two at a time into the shade beside the shed and sitting cross-legged on the ground. Books: mainly children's and young adults'. Toys: Barbie and Ken, stuffed animals. I was particularly taken with a floppy-eared dog with one blue and one green eye.

"That's Towser," Rob's voice said from behind me. "Caro used to drag him everyplace."

"Why the different-colored eyes?"

"The other blue one got lost, and the best my mother could find was a green one."

"Interesting. Your mother didn't strike me as someone who would try to repair a toy."

"She wasn't always as bad as she is now."

"Your parents took me to lunch. They didn't seem to be very…nurturing."

A shadow fell across his face. "It all goes back to Marissa. The unplanned but much-beloved baby. Their world as they knew it ended the day I shot her."

"Rob…"

"No. I've come to terms with it; accidents happen. But I will never come to terms with my father leaving a loaded gun where a kid could find and use it. I'm not an activist like Caro was, but every incident of an accidental shooting or a disturbed person blasting at others—like the Gabrielle Giffords tragedy, where the asshole took out six people, including a kid—eats at my guts. Don't let me get started on the Kennedys or Martin Luther King. Or the parents who're 'disappointed' with how their lives turned out and kill their entire families and themselves. Themselves, okay, if they want to end it. But nobody should get to decide who deserves to live or die. No-body."

I stood up and hefted the two boxes. "Judges and juries do that all the time. It's called 'due process of law.'"

He took the boxes from me and moved toward the door of the storage unit. "But is a panel of twelve people—some of whom are thinking about the work time and wages they're losing and others who are bored or consider themselves modern-day Sherlock Holmeses—do they really qualify to make life-or-death decisions?"

"No. But it's what we've got, take it or leave it."

He dumped the boxes outside the unit and came back with three more. "I'd prefer to leave it."

Actually, when I considered the issue, I did too. I've been a witness in court cases so often that—with a few exceptions—they all blur together. I've also been a juror, and I've noticed how the process of deliberation can get cut short, depending on how desperate the members of the panel are to get home to their families.

I sat down and started on the first box Rob had brought out. More toys, postcards, souvenirs.

After a moment I addressed the issue we'd been discussing. "I've made that decision myself—who gets to live or die. I shot a man who was trying to kill my best friend. I shot a man who had his gun sights trained on my husband. I just did it—in a situation like that, there's no time for philosophical argument."

"And you're at peace with what you did?"

"No. I still have nightmares."

"But you'd do the same thing again?"

"In a heartbeat."

After a moment he said, "I get it. But what I did—"

"Was primarily your father's fault. As my husband says,

guns are not for everyone. Especially for a person who leaves a loaded one where a child can get his hands on it. I'm surprised your father wasn't prosecuted. People usually are."

"My father had connections. The whole thing just went away. Sort of like the memory of Marissa."

"But *you* didn't forget."

"I think about it every day of my life. I try to justify it as an accident. It doesn't help; I still wake up crying. I've never married, never even had a significant relationship. I bury myself in my work, and don't get close to my colleagues. Shit, there was this dog I wanted to adopt a couple of years ago, but I couldn't."

"Because you're afraid you'll hurt somebody—or something—again."

"…I guess."

"You *know*." I opened the second box. Junior high school stuff—yearbooks, a cheerleading pom-pom, photographs of a picnic on a beach, a champagne cork that must have commemorated a special, perhaps clandestine occasion.

Rob sat down on the other side of the box.

"What was Marissa like?" I asked.

His dark gaze lightened. "A happy baby. Well, not exactly a baby—she was four years old.…" His voice broke and he coughed. "She was delighted with everything: learning—she could read by age three. Animals at the zoo—she wanted to know all about them. Sailing—back then we had a small boat that we took out on the Bay. She was advanced for her age: sometimes she'd sneak into our parents' bedroom and experiment with Mom's makeup—

with disastrous results, of course. And like Patty, she loved to plant things and watch them grow. One summer—"

He broke off, covered his eyes, from which tears had started leaking.

I touched his arm. "Rob, Marissa had a happy life."

"But I shortened it—"

"You, yes. But it could have been somebody or something else. She could've run out into traffic and been hit by a car. She could've come down with a disease and died. She could've lived into her teens, gotten into bad company, and overdosed. Thing is, length doesn't matter. Quality does."

He pulled his arm away from my hand. "And you think I should ramp up the quality of my life? Pretend none of this awfulness happened?"

"I can't imagine what you should do. You lost Marissa, you lost Caro, and your parents are assholes. But you still have Patty, and she needs you. I expect you need her too."

He sat silent for a long time, his head bowed. Then he said, "Right. Let's go through the rest of these boxes, and then I'll go over to Oakland and take Patty out to dinner."

6:55 p.m.

"Wait a minute," Rob said. "What's that?"

The outside light had waned and the temperature had cooled. We'd moved into the storage unit and sat down under the single bare bulb.

"What's what?" I asked.

"That photograph."

I'd found it in an envelope that had apparently slipped and stuck between the cabinet and the wall. I'd scarcely had time to look at it, but I handed it to him.

"Amelia and some woman I've never seen before."

I took it back and studied it. The two women appeared to be clowning around, mugging for the camera. In the background were forested hills, and in the foreground was a shadow—the person who'd taken the picture and, from his size, most likely a man.

"Does this background look familiar to you?"

He shook his head. "It could be anyplace in California. Anyplace in any number of states."

"This woman"—I jabbed my fingertip at the unidentified one—"are you sure you've never seen her? Maybe she was a friend of Caro's?"

"Probably, since her picture's in this storage unit. But I'm sure I'd recognize her if she had been."

I looked at the woman again: long dark hair pulled back into a raggedy ponytail; wide mouth; deep tan; very white teeth. She looked vaguely familiar, but I couldn't place her. Probably, with her regular features, I'd recognized her as a type, rather than an individual.

"May I keep this?" I asked Rob.

"Sure, why not? It's nothing to me."

9:16 p.m.

I still hadn't had my talk with Jill Starkey. The woman had an unreasonable bias against Caro Warrick, and I wanted to know why. Also, she might have knowledge about the case that hadn't turned up in the voluminous files I'd viewed.

A light mist was gathering when I parked half a block from her building and, after receiving no answer to my several rings, I decided to stake it out rather than relinquish a rare and coveted space in such a congested area.

I didn't waste the time, either. I used both my laptop and my cell phone. Mick had been in touch: he'd accessed Caro's landline bills and found two calls the week before last to a number that had turned out to be Dave and Kayla Walden's. So much for them not knowing her.

I'd learned through Inspector Devlin Fast—again he was working the night shift—that James Bettencourt's conviction for assault with a deadly weapon stemmed from his smacking a fellow diner in the face with a wine bottle at one of the Financial district's better restaurants, after the man cast aspersions upon Bettencourt's deceased daughter. The victim, one Robert Frasier, had sustained severe cuts and a lacerated eyelid, but acknowledged that he had provoked Bettencourt, and the presiding judge had given Amelia's father two years' probation. Bettencourt had served his probation with no further incident and then moved south. Fast had an address and phone number for him, and I wrote them down, just in case.

Both Mick and I had been working on putting together background on Jill Starkey. As usual, his was more comprehensive than mine. A native of Indiana, Starkey had received her BA in journalism at Northwestern University in Illinois and, during the short-lived boom years of newspaper hiring, moved west to work at the *Chronicle*—first as a general assignment reporter, next as a crime and trial reporter, and finally as a columnist. Mick's research implied that it was her particularly venomous coverage of the Warrick trial that had elevated her to columnist-everybody-loves-to-hate.

Unlike most journalists, however, Starkey embroidered the truth when it suited her purposes. A particularly vicious and largely false column about connections between a prominent and respected San Francisco family and a South American drug lord had resulted in a libel suit and hefty settlement levied upon the *Chron*, and put her out of a job. Starkey rebounded, borrowing money from "friends and admirers" and founding *The Right Shoe*. Judging from its offices and circulation figures—which Mick provided me—none of those loans had been repaid.

"Look," I said, "why don't you tackle Starkey? You're more familiar with her history and besides, she hates me."

TUESDAY, JANUARY 10

5:50 a.m.

I'd gone to bed early and slept soundly. Now the phone shrilled close to my ear. I'd left it on my pillow last night after talking with Hy.

I turned my head so I could see the clock and sighed. At this hour the call could only be: 1) a dire emergency; 2) a bright-eyed and bushy-tailed telemarketer; 3) a wrong number; or 4) Ma. Of the options, I hoped it was a telemarketer. At least they were used to being hung up on.

But it was none of the above. Instead, Inspector Devlin Fast. This was one contact I couldn't risk alienating by shouting at him, so in a modulated tone I asked, "Don't you ever sleep?"

"Normally, two or three hours. But the information you requested came in by text from an inspector on the early shift a few minutes ago, and I thought you'd like to know."

"Information? Oh, right." The names of the other two investigators Caro Warrick had hired.

"Got something to write on?"

I grabbed a pen and scratch pad from the nightstand. "Go ahead."

"Hamilton Roth, works out of an office on Polk Street." He gave me the address and phone number. "Then there's Edna Sheep—"

"You're kidding me."

"What's the matter with the name?"

"Nothing." I couldn't explain to him that on one of his recent trips to London Hy, as a joke, had brought me back an inflatable sex toy called Edna the Party Sheep. "It's unusual, that's all. You have contact information for her?"

"Only an e-mail address." He read it to me.

"Odd, for someone in the business."

"Maybe she's paranoid."

"Or hearing impaired. Or mute."

"More likely she prefers to screen her potential clients."

"Well, given some of the potentials who have wandered into my agency's offices recently, I can't fault her for that."

"Speaking of offices," Fast said, "where are you hanging your hat since the elevator crash?"

"RI's building."

"Nice. You planning to stay?"

"Haven't decided yet. We've got a huge caseload, and a couple of the operatives are away on winter vacations."

"Where I'd like to go. Hawaii, Mexico…Keep me posted. I'll be here."

I switched off the phone and flopped back onto the pillows. No use trying to go back to sleep, that wasn't going to happen. Too early to call Hamilton Roth. But I could e-mail Edna Sheep. I reached for my robe, staggered up the spiral staircase and along to the kitchen— and realized I was out of coffee. The cats twined around my legs, mowling for food. Thank God I hadn't used up all of *that*; they'd probably have ripped my throat out. I fed them, settled for some Rise 'n Shine tea that somebody had given me last Christmas, and fired off a message to the Sheep woman.

She got back to me immediately by phone.

"Another female private investigator, and an insomniac like me!" she exclaimed. "Aren't you the Sharon McCone I read about in connection with those awful bombings? And then you were shot in the head—"

"Yes, that's me." I ran my hand through the tangled hair on said head, then leaned heavily on the table. People who are cheerful before eight in the morning exhaust me. Maybe I should've stayed in bed after all.

Edna Sheep wasn't going to allow that, though. She said, "I'd be delighted to talk with you about the Warrick case. Over breakfast? I know a delightful little place near Embarcadero Center. Exquisite omelets and crepes—"

My head started to throb as if I had a hangover, but that couldn't be—I'd had only one glass of wine last night. It was obvious that I was developing an allergy to Edna Sheep even before I'd met her.

"Sounds lovely," I forced out. "What time?"

"Oh, as soon as possible. It's wonderful to make the acquaintance of another morning person."

7:20 a.m.

The "delightful place" near the Embarcadero Center wasn't any such thing. Situated between two elegant highrises, it was a seventies-style storefront that exuded greasy smells and whose counters were defaced with crude carvings, its fake leather booths slashed—probably in vengeance for the quality of the food.

Edna Sheep was waiting for me in the extreme rear booth, a cup of coffee in front of her. Upon first glimpse she looked like your average office worker—loosely permed gray-brown hair, carefully applied makeup, casual business attire.

But then she opened her mouth and bleated.

Honest to God, she *bleated*!

"That's my signature greeting," she told me, sliding a business card across the table.

Nobody in the coffee shop was paying attention to us. They must've heard it all before. I looked at the card: on its bottom left-hand side was a cartoon of a fluffy sheep; a voice balloon over its head proclaimed, "Ewe'll love the Sheep Agency!"

Oh my God...

"What'll it be?" Edna asked. "Eggs Benedict? Crepes? Blueberry pancakes?"

"Uh, coffee and toast, please."

"Cheap date," she said, motioning to the waitress, who took our orders and departed. "I've made you copies of my files on..." She looked around, narrowing her eyes at the other diners. "On you know, what's-her-name."

Why the subterfuge? I wondered as she shoved two thick envelopes toward me. If no one had noticed her bleat, it was unlikely that they'd eavesdrop on our conversation.

I decided to build fellowship by colluding in her secretiveness. "I'll go over these later, but what was your impression of...the subject?"

"Guilty as hell."

"But you took her on as a client—"

"Because I've got a heavy-duty mortgage and a son in Palm Springs who thinks he's a golf pro but is really a waiter and is always asking me for money."

Another reason I was glad I'd never had children.

"What made you so sure of Warrick's guilt?" I asked.

"Well, it was such an odd request—that I affirm her acquittal. As if she'd committed the crime and wanted to make sure she'd gotten off scot-free."

"Double jeopardy—"

"That was another warning signal. No matter what I turned up, she couldn't be tried again."

"But she could be vilified in the press, cast out by friends and family."

"Not with the confidentiality agreement she made me sign. Extensive. Ironclad."

Caro had not asked me to sign such a document. She'd been forthcoming, wanting me to look into the most private areas of her life. But maybe, after she'd had a look at Edna Sheep—

Our food came. Sheep dug into her Mexican scramble with gusto. Reached for the saltshaker and added at least a teaspoon of the stuff, then chomped onward.

I asked, "Did you know Caro hired another investigator after you told her you couldn't help?"

"Ham-and-Eggs Roth? Yeah, I recommended him."

"Why?"

"Because he's an extremely practical man, and I thought he could talk some sense into her."

"And did he?"

"No. He fell for her line of bullshit—fell hard."

"In what way?"

"You'd best ask him, Ms. McCone. Me, I try to stay out of things like that."

12:05 p.m.

I understood why Edna had called the other investigator "Ham-and-Eggs" Roth. He was ovoid, with little feet and a small, pointed head, and in between—well, "ham" was a polite way to describe his physique. But he welcomed me warmly at a very good café near his offices on Polk Street close to the Civic Center, and the first thing he said was "I've admired your work for years."

Flattery—I fall for it every time.

"I'm surprised we've never met," I responded. "Do you attend any of the industry conventions?"

He shook his head. "I'm semiretired. I keep my license current and occasionally take on jobs for clients who really need my help, but I avoid large gatherings. My cases are low-key, mostly civil, and I like it that way. But you— you just keep coming on strong."

"Thank you."

"You mentioned that you'd had breakfast with our colleague Edna Sheep," Ham said. "Since I know the quality of the eating places she frequents, I've taken the liberty of alerting the kitchen to prepare an exceptionally good meal for you. IPAs for both of us should be along in a minute."

"Oh, thank you. Breakfast with Edna—"

"Sucked."

"Exactly." I paused as the waiter set down our mugs of beer, then asked, "She said you fell for Caro's 'line of bull-shit' hard. What did that mean?"

"I recognized the truth when I heard it."

"But why did you agree to investigate the case after the fact? She'd been acquitted, couldn't be retried."

He raised his mug to me, drank, and said, "That should be apparent to one of your analytical expertise."

"Because she wasn't guilty, and you thought by taking on the job, you'd discover who was."

He nodded.

"But you didn't."

"I was close, but then Caro herself cut me off and wouldn't listen to what I was trying to tell her."

"And what was that?"

"It's a very long and complicated story...."

3:45 p.m.

On the way back to the office, I thought over what Ham Roth had revealed to me, trying to put the story into some logical order.

It wouldn't take shape.

After Caro's arrest for Amelia's murder, she'd retained Ned Springer—a logical choice since they'd been friends since childhood. At Caro's request, after she was acquitted, Springer suggested she hire Edna Sheep. When Sheep didn't work out, she recommended Caro try Ham Roth.

"Edna's good at what she does," Roth had told me. "Civil matters, little stuff, but a murder case was far beyond her capabilities. I dug deeper."

"And found?"

"Inconsistencies and downright cover-ups. Amelia had been seen the night before she died in a Mission district club, the Crazy Eights, with an unidentified man—not her boyfriend, Jake Green. They appeared to be quarreling. Caro initially told investigators that she had letters from Amelia admitting she was also having an affair with an unnamed married man but, when asked, she couldn't produce them and then claimed Amelia must have meant a divorced man. Another friend of Amelia said she'd told her she was afraid during the last week of her life: she'd received threatening phone calls and had been chased down the street by a man in a black cape."

"Melodrama?"

"Amelia had a tendency toward that, yes. But according to a couple of other friends, the fear seemed genuine, and she was planning to move away from the city and start over."

"These friends of hers who claimed Amelia felt threatened and afraid—who were they?"

He shrugged. "I'll have my assistant go through the file and e-mail you the list."

"I've gone over the trial transcripts and spoken with Ned Springer. Not a lot of what you've told me came out."

"The prosecutor thought he had an open-and-shut case. He didn't investigate much or call the right witnesses and, for all his inexperience, Springer was smart enough not to complicate the issues."

"And you?"

"Ms. McCone, you and I discover facts; we put them into the right hands and hope justice will be done. And that's the end of it."

Maybe for him, but not for me.

7:16 p.m.

"So," I said to Mick, "d'you want to go clubbing with me or don't you?"

"Shar, we'd look ridiculous. I'm young enough to be your son."

"Are not!"

"Am too!"

"You can always pretend you're out with a cougar."

"Hate that term."

"Me too, but I really need—"

"Why don't you ask Derek?"

Derek Ford: my handsome, stylish, Eurasian operative. Perfect.

Mick added, "He hangs around the clubs all the time, and he's been known to date older women."

"You keep calling me 'older' and you'll pay for it, Savage."

"No, but *you'll* have to pay Derek overtime."

10:15 p.m.

The club scene was just beginning to warm up, Derek told me.

He suggested we hit the Mission district first. "The Tenderloin's getting trendy, but it's safer there after all the winos pass out. North Beach's strictly for tourists or foodies who've discovered restaurants like Don Pisto's or Le Bordeaux."

"Including you, I assume?" Derek had been known to frequent the most popular—to say nothing of expensive—restaurants in town.

"Sure. I'm not embarrassed by being a foodie." He smiled easily and made a U-turn on my narrow block at the tail end of Church Street.

"Nice turning radius," I commented.

"Not as good as your BMW. But this old clunker does what I tell it to."

The "old clunker" was a red 1969 Porsche 912, fully restored.

"You've read the files on the case?" I asked.

"Skimmed them, but I've picked up on the essentials."

"What're the odds that anybody we meet tonight will remember Amelia Bettencourt or Caro Warrick?"

"Well, the clubs and patrons change all the time but, given such a high-profile murder case, I'd say some people will recall them. Or claim to. What we need is to weed out the people who're seeking their fifteen seconds of fame from those who might actually have something for us. Bartenders are usually the best witnesses: they see and hear more than anybody else. Of course, they charge for information."

"Wyatt House will be more than happy to cover the bill. And we'll tell people that if the publisher later on finds out they lied, they'll sue their asses off."

Derek grinned at me and screeched around the corner of Church and Eighteenth Streets. "I like the way you think, boss." He paused. "By the way, I don't know if you've read any of the coverage on the club scene being dangerous."

"Muggings, stabbings, attempted rape, yeah."

"Well, that's pretty much changed. Last year the cops put the screws to the club owners and beefed up street patrols. By now the scene's safer than your own mother's living room."

A lot safer, considering some of the tirades I've been subjected to at Ma's.

10:31 p.m.

"Do you know what she said to me? 'I could love him if he wasn't so fat.'"

"Well fat's kind of out right now...."

"Absinthe. I know a great little shop that stocks it. What you do, is pour it over a sugar cube—"

"Drugs're too easy to get hold of these days. They've kind of lost their charm."

"I don't know, they still charm me."

I rolled my eyes at Derek and, smiling, he twirled me around the dance floor. We were at our second club, Mobius, having struck out at the Crazy Eights, where Amelia had gone the night before she was murdered.

"He's cute, and I love that tat of scorpions around his neck, but what's he doing with her?"

Derek mumbled into my ear, "You know, I regret ever getting this tat; it hurt, but they say it *really* hurts to remove one."

"*What's wrong with her?*"

"*She's old.*"

"*I think she's hot.*"

"*You would.*"

Derek pulled me closer. "I think you're hot, boss, really hot."

"I'd like to slug that woman."

"Stay calm. Before this set ends, we'll go talk with the bartender."

"But she said I was *old*! And Mick said the same thing earlier today."

"You're Mick's aunt; you'll always seem old to him—even when *he's* old. As for that woman, she's stupid and insecure, reacting to that gray streak in your hair. How long have you had it?"

"Since high school. I used to dye it, but then I realized I was getting into some ageist, sexist thing and stopped. Now I'm kind of fond of it."

"Does it make you feel old?"

"No."

"What does?"

"People saying I'm old."

Derek threw his head back and laughed so loudly that the couples near us stared. "And since when has what other people say mattered to you?"

"Well, in third grade, this asshole kid named Petey called me a 'dirty Injun,' so I beat him up and got a week of detention."

"Geez, it's a wonder you didn't take your case to the ACLU."

"Us 'Injuns' weren't as trendy back then as we are now."

Derek twirled me around once more and began ushering me off the floor. "Bartender's not too busy right now. Let's corner him."

The bartender was mixing drinks in a cocktail shaker. He looked up and grinned when Derek said, "Hey, Don."

"Ford, my man! Haven't seen you in a while. Who's your lady friend?"

"She's a friend, but also my boss. Sharon McCone. We're working a case together."

Don shook hands with me, then asked, "Does that mean you can't have a drink—on the house?"

I said, "I'd love a glass of chardonnay. We're not as strict about drinking on duty as the cops are."

"Ford?"

"Same."

"Let me deliver this batch of apricot sunsets—good Christ, what is the drinking world coming to?—and I'll be right back at you."

I looked at Derek. "Well known man-about-town, are you?"

"You know me, Shar; I love the night life and now, thanks to SavageFor, I can afford it."

SavageFor.com was a real-time search engine that Derek and Mick had created. Last year they'd sold out to Omnivore for a sum that would've allowed either of them never to work again in his lifetime. Mick persisted, because he loved detecting, but I was seriously afraid of losing Derek, who loved to play.

I said, "I've been meaning to ask you—"

"No, I don't drink apricot sunsets or any of those concoctions with funny names."

"Actually, it's about—"

The bartender returned with our wine. As he set the glasses down he said, "You're on a case. Must have something to do with this club."

"Right," I told him. "Three years ago on October twenty-first a woman named Amelia Bettencourt may have come in here with an unidentified man—"

"And the next night, her best friend killed her," he finished for me. "But I never bought that. If it had been the other way, maybe."

"Why do you say that?"

"I knew both girls. Amelia was always flashing around, trying to attract guys, with never a thought for Caro. But Caro, she was even more stunning to men, and genuinely cared for Amelia. If any guy hurt Amelia, he was just off Caro's radar screen forever. Loyalty like that you don't see much in the dating scene. Or many other places, come to think of it. There was no way Caro would've viciously murdered Amelia over that slimy snake Jake Green."

"'Slimy snake?'"

"You met him?"

"Yes. He seemed...kind of sleazy, but—"

Don gave me a conspiratorial wink and motioned me closer. "Let me give you the real skinny on Jake Green."

A patron signaled him from the other end of the bar. "My relief's coming on in five minutes. Grab that booth over there, and I'll join you."

11:02 p.m.

Don slid into the booth next to me, and another round of drinks immediately appeared. Derek and I reached for our wallets, but Don shook his head. "Your money's no good in my place."

"You own the club?" I asked.

"This and two others. But I like to keep my hand in at tending bar."

I smiled. "I own my agency and could put in a few hours a day behind my desk, but I like to keep my hand in at active investigation."

"Good woman. I like that. Then there's the playboy here—"

"Hey," Derek said, "I work!"

"Only because your father made that a condition in his will."

Now this was new information. I looked questioningly at Derek. "We'll discuss that later," he said. Added to Don, "About Jake Green...?"

"He was in here three, maybe four times a week. At first with Carolyn Warrick and then with Amelia Bettencourt. Beautiful girls, but they were an intentional distraction."

"From what?" I asked.

"His real business—laundering money. This is the Mission, right? Lots of Latinos, Hispanics, whatever they're calling themselves now. You can't tell who's a legit worker with a mortgage and two kids to support from somebody with 'assets' he or she wants to move. The music, the dancing, the booze can cover up a lot of action."

"And you permit this?" Derek asked.

"You want to stay in your business, kid, you better get real. Take me: Do I want this building burned to the ground? Or one of my employees raped or shot in the restroom? Do I want somebody following me home and posing a threat to my wife and kids? It's a bad bargain, but I leave them alone, they leave me alone."

"I get you."

I knew a fair amount about money laundering, especially of the type that involved funneling funds into offshore banks that adhered to more stringent secrecy requirements than those in the US—primarily because Hy had been involved in a case the year before that dealt with the changing regulations within the Swiss banking community. It had revealed large-scale fraud, but how much illicit cash could be moved by a shoddy travel agent who met his clients in a Mission district bar?

Don must've seen the skeptical look on my face, because he said, "There's a lot more money moving through this place than you'd think. And Sleazy Green's in a perfect position to make it happen. Travel agent, lots of freebies from the airlines, lots of connections with the personnel and flight crews. Even with the increased security, if there's a will, there's a way."

I nodded, thinking of Hy's many stories about the mechanics of executive protection and hostage retrieval, especially the time when he'd taken a wrongly convicted— and stupid—American man out of Saudi Arabia by hiding him between the skin and the interior of a plane. I'd have to discuss this situation with him.

Don took out a card and scribbled on it. "My home number, if you can't reach me at any of my clubs." Then he stood and gestured to the waitress. "Another round for my friends, please."

"Interesting guy," Derek said.

"Mmm."

"What?"

"Some connection between money laundering and gun control that I can't quite make. Probably because of *that*." I pointed to the glass of wine that had just been set in front of me.

"Hey, boss, you losing your drinking capacity?"

"That's dangerously close to an old-person comment, son."

"Don't call me 'son.'"

"Why not?"

"Because I've already got a Mommie Dearest. I don't need another."

WEDNESDAY, JANUARY 11

6:31 a.m.

Rain, slapping down on the deck above my bedroom. More god-awful January weather. I buried
my head under my pillow, squeezed my eyes closed.
Maybe if I concentrated really hard, I'd open them to a
sunny April day.

Of course, I'd also have to close my ears, and I'd never
figured out how to do that.

Well, I was awake now, no reason not to get on with the
day's business. I picked up the phone and called Hy in LA;
he sounded alert, had probably been up for hours.

At the sound of his voice, I felt a lonely pang; I knew he
was feeling it too, because his tone changed, became lower
and more intimate.

"How you doing?" he asked.

"…Okay."

"Just okay?"

"Yeah. You?"

"Tired. Disappointed that I'm not going to be able to
make it home tonight."

"No?" The lonely feeling intensified.

"No. I'll probably have to— Well, anyway, what've you been doing?"

"I had some unpleasant reminders of my own mortality last night."

"McCone, what happened?"

God, I shouldn't have phrased it that way! It hadn't been all that long since I'd been shot.

"Nothing important," I said quickly. "I went clubbing with Derek."

"Clubbing? *You?*"

"Because of this Warrick case."

"And how did that lead to reminders of your mortality?"

"People in the clubs thought I was too old."

A relieved silence. Then Hy laughed. "Well, face it, darlin'—we're both a *little* old."

"Thanks."

"Whoops—this *has* gotten you grumpy."

"I'm just grumpy in general lately."

"Well, I'll have to hurry up and get back there. Give you something to really feel grumpy about."

I smiled at the teasing note in his voice. "Never."

"Never?"

"Nope."

A small silence filled the miles between us. Then I said, "I need to tap into your expertise."

"I thought I sensed an agenda behind this call."

"No agenda—I just missed you. But now that we're talking—refresh my memory on the basics of money laundering."

"What next?" His voice was amused. "Okay, money

laundering. Conversion of ill-gotten gains to seemingly licit ones. There are five basic types: bank methods, smurfing, bulk cash smuggling, currency exchanges, and double-invoicing. Bank methods usually involve gaining a controlling interest in a financial institution and then moving the money through it. Smurfing is when cash is broken down into small amounts in order to avoid suspicion; bearer instruments, such as money orders, are used. Bulk cash smuggling: physically moving the cash to a bank in a country where secrecy requirements are greater than normal."

"What I'm looking at is probably bulk cash smuggling, since the suspect has strong connections within the travel industry."

"I'm assuming this cash is leaving, rather than entering, the US."

"Right."

"Our preventative laws have been in place since the mideighties. Cash withdrawals over ten thousand dollars have to be noted on a currency transaction report that identifies the person who made the withdrawal and the source of the money to the US Treasury. However, a person can make as many withdrawals as he or she wants under that amount from any number of financial institutions and not alert the feds. Or if the funds were received as cash and never deposited anywhere, the launderers just slip them into the old suitcase and go."

"Airport screening—"

"Is not all it's made out to be in the press. Flight-crew members aren't under heavy scrutiny. People who fly the same route with the same airline on a regular basis aren't either. Then you've got your private jets like RI's; they don't have as much range as commercial airliners, but they'll get you across the borders. As of last year, security screeners seemed more interested in passengers' inappropriate dress than smuggled cash."

I smiled wryly, remembering the college athlete who was banned from his flight because his pants were at half-mast.

"You say you have a suspect?" Hy asked.

"A travel agent."

"What's the source of the money?"

"I'm not sure. I have a suspicion, but I'm going to have to dig deeper."

"Not ready to share, huh?"

"You know me—I like to be right before I tell all."

8:55 a.m.

When I got to the office, Mick handed me a file. "The deep background you asked me for."

The file was thick. "You must've stayed up all night gathering this."

"Not with the equipment I've got at home. I slept like a baby while this was coming in and printing out."

"What about Jill Starkey? Are you keeping tabs on her?"

"She went to some newspaper columnists' convention in Seattle yesterday. I've got an op from the Brent Agency monitoring her."

Thank God Wyatt House was paying for this investigation!

"Good work," I said, and moved on to my office.

As before, I was overwhelmed by the luxury of the space. I suspected Hy's hand in this—a subtle lure to make me consent to the consolidation of our agencies. Well, it just might work.

The deep background information turned up a few facts that were interesting or downright amusing, but nothing of any real import.

Edna Sheep's real name was Edna Finklesheep. She'd had it legally changed nineteen years ago. Well, no wonder.

Jill Starkey had been raped in her junior year of college; the rapist had been acquitted. She'd received extensive counseling from a therapist who was a member of the NRA. That explained her anger and her support of gun ownership.

Jake Green had bought a two-million-dollar home in Atherton, the expensive enclave on the Peninsula, three years ago. Money laundering yielded large profits.

Betsy Warrick—née Ames—had climbed a streetlight pole on Telegraph Avenue during the anti–Vietnam War protests at Berkeley and hurled water balloons at the police. They'd had to drag her down kicking and screaming. Her fiancé, Ben Warrick, had bailed her out.

Betsy, Betsy. Knowing you now, who would've thought?

Dave Walden had been an Eagle Scout and won a blue ribbon for his pygmy goat at the Sonoma County Fair when he was sixteen. Kayla Walden frequently visited a prominent plastic surgeon in Greenbrae, Marin County. Jethro Weatherford had spent two nights in jail for public drunkenness fifteen years ago; the authorities had then decided to leave him alone because he had walked on the proper side of the road, hadn't stumbled, and hadn't disturbed anyone.

And then came the biggie: a post on a cold case site from someone calling himself "RadioactiveMac."

> SF PI Sharon McCone has been hired by exonerated killer Caro Warrick to reinvestigate the murder of Amelia Bettencourt. Warrick's dead now. McCone had a big fall. She's next.

I ripped the page from the report, rushed down the hallway, and stamped into Mick's office. "Did you think this was funny?" I asked, thrusting the page at him.

He scanned it, frowning. "I didn't read it before I gave it to you. Do you think it's serious?"

"Could be. Who the hell is RadioactiveMac?"

"I don't know, but I can find out." He swiveled around to his keyboard and began tapping out his magic on it.

I sat down on the corner of his desk, fidgeting and poking at a chipped fingernail. After a few minutes Mick said, "This is proving to be more difficult than I thought. The name leads to others, which in turn lead to still more. A typical way of disguising your identity."

"But you *can* find out?"

"In time."

"How much time?"

"Within the hour. I'm going to run a couple of very reliable searches." He swiveled back, did more magic. "I'll let you know when I've got something. What's this in his message about you having a big fall?"

"The elevator crash. This guy is probably responsible for it."

"Shit!" He swiveled back toward me, eyes wide.

I said, "While we're waiting, I need to talk to you about Derek."

"What'd he do—put the moves on you last night?"

"This is serious. I'm afraid we're going to lose him. He doesn't need the job or the money, and he likes to play."

Mick laughed. "He does need both the job and the money. Derek's a trust-fund baby, yeah, but there's a provision in the trust that'll keep him on the job."

"What provision?"

"His grandparents were immigrants who were interned during World War II—at Tule Lake, I think. They had one kid, a daughter. After they were released, they moved here to the city, lived dirt-poor while the grandfather established a number of produce stands that mainly catered to the Japanese. The daughter married a Vietnam vet, Martin Ford, who had a lot of business smarts. He turned the produce stands into Fresh to You."

That was a nationwide chain of high-end grocery stores. "No wonder Derek's got a trust fund."

Mick nodded. "And a lot of hard work went into establishing it. From what Derek's told me, his father disapproved of his tendencies to play and overspend, so the trust only pays out basic living expenses—adjusted occasionally for inflation—and requires him to work at something 'meaningful' till he's forty-five."

"But SavageFor—" The real-time search engine he and Derek had developed in the days when such sites were almost unheard of.

"We sold it to Omnivore, remember? And creating it was just noodling around, not working."

"Still, what you got for it would be enough for him to live on."

"Not with his expensive tastes. And I've got a feeling they're only going to get more expensive as he ages. By the time he gets his hands on the money he'll be ready for a string of trophy wives and multiple vacation homes."

"Kind of a harsh thing to say about your friend."

"Nah, money's not all that Derek's about. He's loyal, generous, and he'd put his life on the line for people he cares about. And that includes you."

"So you don't think we'll lose him?"

"He enjoys the work so, no, not till his forty-fifth birthday—and then he'll probably fly us all to Paris for dinner."

Mick's computer beeped. He turned to it and said, "Well, well."

"What?" I leaned forward to look, but couldn't make out what was on the screen.

"RadioactiveMac is someone we know."

"Who?"

"Do you remember a guy named Daniel Winters?"

11:23 a.m.

I sat in my armchair reviewing the file on Daniel Winters.

He'd come to us as a client two years ago. A middle-aged archaeologist from Berkeley who had amassed a valuable collection of East African artifacts. He'd noticed certain objects missing, and suspected a household employee was stealing them. The employee, a housekeeper, had not returned to work the day after he questioned her. The normal procedure in such cases is to check with pawnbrokers and antique shops that don't require proof of ownership or provenance—which I did, with no result. Then I received a tip from a high-end jeweler who had once been our client that Daniel Winters himself had been selling the artifacts to various unscrupulous dealers across a tristate area. He was overconfident enough in his ability to outwit me (and/or misinformed enough about my skills) to think I would help him, but I ended up turning him in myself.

Winters had escaped prosecution by fleeing the country; now, apparently, he was back.

He was back, and I was back in the news because of the Warrick case. A perfect reminder for him to harass me for exposing his crimes.

I wasn't too worried about Winters. He'd never exhibited signs of violence; annoying messages were more his style. Still, I called the officer at the SFPD who'd handled the case and then copied and forwarded her the post. The department would be on the lookout now, since Winters was still a fugitive.

God, what a morning! The day, I decided, could only get worse.

2:30 p.m.

And it did.

Hy called: all hell had broken loose in an African country I'd never heard of, and a client, CEO of an American construction company working there, had been taken hostage. Hy was at Kennedy Airport in New York, awaiting his flight. He'd phone again when he changed planes in Johannesburg.

Ted went home early with symptoms of the flu that was ravaging the city's population.

Julia Rafael, my only Spanish-speaking operative and a single mother, had had to bring her son, Tonio, to work after he finished preschool since her sister, who usually took care of him, had the same flu. He was a lively, bright child, and I loved him dearly, but his running down the hallway and bursting into my office drove me to distraction. Julia had nerves of steel when it came to her work, but by noon his behavior had her clawing at her beautiful, upswept black hair. She released it from its tortoiseshell comb and let it fall to her shoulders. Said to me, "Sometimes I think I should've stayed on the streets instead of having a kid and going legit."

The remark didn't surprise me; Julia was brutally honest about her past as a teenage hooker in the Mission district.

My operative Adah Joslyn, whom I'd lured away from the SFPD Homicide squad, phoned to say she and her husband Craig Morland—also lured away, but in his case from the FBI—were also flu sufferers. Why did newly married people always have to do things together?

It started raining again—pouring, actually.

And when I went down to the garage, I found that someone had backed into the Z-4 and broken its taillight.

I got into the car, pressed my forehead against the steering wheel, and wished for speedy recoveries and ongoing good health for those I knew and loved. And for anybody else who needed good wishes. Then I started to wish for Hy and me—that he'd be safe and return soon. I'd often thought of our lives as strange and dangerous, but this deep a concern had never really touched me at the core, as it did tonight.

My cell trilled—some melody Jamie had programmed in that I didn't like but kept forgetting to replace with a normal ring tone. Hy? No, impossible that he'd have arrived in Johannesburg by now. I answered, and for a moment there was silence.

Then a muffled voice said, "You know the Presidio?"

"More or less." Given its size, it's impossible to know it all.

"The Chapel of Our Lady?"

A small, white Civil War–era church tucked into the trees near the center of the former military base. I'd been there for a wedding a few years ago. "I can find it."

"Be there. Eight thirty. Come alone."

Jesus, had I suddenly morphed into a character in a forties B minus movie?

"Who is this?" I demanded.

"Somebody who can help you—eight thirty. Be prompt."

"What's this about—?" But the person hung up.

Male? Female? I couldn't tell.

Chapel of Our Lady: unused at this time on a Wednesday night, but not necessarily a dangerous place, due to its proximity to other buildings such as the old Officers' Club.

An anonymous caller who claimed he could help me? Pretty unlikely.

Come alone? No way.

I should ignore the call. A prank, that was all it was. Maybe.

But how many people had my cellular number? Well, too many. I'd have to consider keeping this one for business and getting another for personal calls.

But for now…

7:55 p.m.

The Presidio of San Francisco has been part of the Golden Gate National Recreation Area since 1994, when the army turned it over to the National Park Service. An active military base since 1776, when it was established to defend San Francisco Bay and Mission Dolores, it passed from Spain to Mexico before becoming a United States outpost south of the Golden Gate. The sprawling acres are mostly wooded, with a scattering of former army buildings that are now devoted to a mix of commercial and public use. Its governing body, the Presidio Trust, has been financially independent since 2006—seven years before the act of Congress stipulated it should be.

The views are spectacular, much of the terrain hilly and fragrant with pine and eucalyptus. It is a place to escape the tensions of the real world, relax and contemplate. It is not a place to wander on a dark winter night, and I didn't intend to stray from my car until my "helpful" caller revealed himself.

Mick—whom I'd brought as backup—and I waited on Moraga Street, within sight of the little chapel. Its white façade gleamed in the outside lights that were focused on it. In spite of the distance I could hear traffic thrumming on the bridge and foghorns bellowing grumpily out to sea. The rain had let up around six o'clock, but the mist was thick. Only one vehicle was parked in the area—a dark van some distance down the block—but there was no one around it.

The absence of people didn't fool me; I knew that in the thickets homeless encampments abounded, sheltering families who had lost their homes in the latest financial debacle and other dispossessed people from all walks of life, many of whom had jobs but nowhere to live. They arose in the morning, cleaned up in the restrooms, and got on with their lives as best they could. They were the unseen, forgotten remnants of our middle class, which soon, if the economy didn't turn around, would be wiped out of existence.

The Presidio was also known as the perfect place for criminals to hide. Mass murderers, drug dealers, and fugitives had sheltered there, as many court transcripts attested. I wasn't about to risk an encounter with any of them.

Beside me, Mick fidgeted. I'd interrupted another of his evenings.

"I know you're annoyed by getting called out on such short notice," I said, "but it's too dangerous for me to come alone."

"I'm not annoyed with *you*."

"Well, you seem that way lately."

He sighed.

"Mick, what's wrong?"

"What isn't?"

"Start with the least annoying and progress up the list."

"One of our neighbors keeps stealing our newspaper."

"So cancel your subscription and go online or watch TV."

"Shar, I may be a techie, but I like the feel of newsprint. Besides, you can't spread out your computer or TV on the kitchen table and dribble jam and spit orange pits on it."

"Then run a surveillance. Trap him or her. They'll be so ashamed they'll never do it again. Next problem."

"This fuckin' economy. Alison's worried about her job."

"Everybody is, especially in the financial sector."

"That's comforting."

"But," I said, drawing the word out, "Hy and I have a financial planner who has twice saved our assets—and asses—by astute moves. I know he'd be thrilled to save yours, too. And if a position suitable for Alison turns up, he'll be sure to put in a good word. I'll give you his card tomorrow."

"Thanks."

"Next problem."

"Both of us hate living in that high-rise, but property like it isn't selling."

"Have you put the condo on the market?"

"No."

"Here's the name and number of a super real-estate agent whom I went to college with." I clicked on the address book on my phone and read the information off to him. "She's the one who represented your dad and Rae when they bought the Sea Cliff place."

"Thanks again. You're the greatest."

No, I wasn't. Those problems were relatively minor. I said, "You're welcome. Next problem—and I expect it's a biggie."

Long pause. "Okay—Alison. She might be pregnant."

I caught my breath. In the dark car, I couldn't see if he was pleased or displeased. "Is that so bad?"

"Shar, you know I love kids, but I'm not ready for that kind of responsibility yet."

"And Alison?"

"She's never wanted any—at least none of her own. Apparently there's some birth defect running through her family."

"What kind of birth defect?"

"I don't know. I don't think she's even sure. One of those things where the family ships the kid off to some home and then never talks about it."

I thought of Marissa Warrick, the damage her siblings suffered because of their parents' inability to acknowledge her death and deal with how it happened. They'd never talked about Marissa again. Alison's family's not coming clean about the birth defect was similar.

I said, "Alison should request medical records, find out."

"I've told her that, but she keeps not getting around to it."

"How far along is she?"

"Nearly two months."

"Missed periods could be caused by stress about the markets, losing her job."

"Don't you think I've tried to tell her that? All she says is that she's been regular like clockwork her whole adult life."

"Has she come to any conclusions about what she's going to do if she is pregnant?"

"She's leaning toward abortion."

"And you?"

"Like I said, I love kids, but this isn't the time. Besides, it's her body, her decision."

"No, it's both of yours. And I sense you have reservations."

"Abortion's such an ugly thing…."

"Mick, nobody really likes the idea of abortion. Oh, I know there are people who have no qualms about it. But in some cases, it can make or break a woman's life."

"Shar, what're you trying to tell me?"

"Unwanted children sense they are unwanted, no matter how the parents try to mask it. Usually they lead troubled lives." I thought about Jamie: she'd told me her mother was into having babies in quantity, and her father was into having groupies. She'd sensed that her conception had happened for complicated and less than desirable reasons; fortunately her innate talent seemed to have saved her. But what of the three younger Little Savages? Maybe they'd escaped the toxic environment in Charlene and Ricky's household in time. They certainly seemed fine, in spite of frequently being shuttled by private jet between home in San Diego and home in San Francisco. But I did sometimes worry about the younger boy, Brian….

Mick said, "Shar, what're you *really* trying to tell me? There's a subtext here that I'm not getting."

It was a secret I'd held close for many years, since my junior year at UC–Berkeley. Only Hy, Hank, and my long-term friend Linnea Carraway knew. I struggled with the words, but my throat closed up. I shuddered, swallowed.

Finally I said, "I had an abortion. In college."

"Oh, Shar—"

"It was the result of a one-night stand. A guy from USC that I would've never gotten near if I'd been sober—but I wasn't. And I was only nineteen; I had nothing to offer a child. But I knew if Ma and Pa found out they'd insist I have it and raise it. Catholics, you know."

"So you…?"

"Yeah. It was a tough decision. I've pretty much put it behind me, but sometimes I wonder…"

"About your life? How it'd have been different? What the kid would've been like? The burdens it would've imposed?"

"All of that. Sometimes I think that I was so selfish."

"Well, maybe you were, and maybe you did the right thing. Think of all the stuff you've done for all the people—"

"That's no excuse."

"Not an excuse, but a reason. The tricky questions in life are all about what and who you are—or want to be. Will you talk to Alison, please? Ease her mind?"

"As soon as she's ready."

We lapsed into silence. Still no one had approached the church, either on foot or by car; the van remained dark. The chapel gleamed pure and white, the cross at its top drawing my gaze.

Was it reproaching me for my actions during that terrible time in college? No, it was simply an inanimate symbol of something I no longer believed in. Actually, I didn't have many clear memories of what I'd gone through only a sense of helplessness, a sense of need, and then a sense of relief. I'd pretty much blocked out the incident. Maybe it was time I dealt with it as a grown woman.

My mother's incessant childbearing—four, and in the middle they'd adopted me. Charlene's similar pattern. My brother John was a good divorced father to his two boys, but my brother Joey had died a junkie, and my youngest sister Patsy now had five children by four different men.

True, Ma was Catholic and there hadn't been as many methods of prevention in her day. You couldn't really blame John's divorce or Joey's addictive personality on growing up in a houseful of kids, but I sometimes wondered if Joey, the quiet but rebellious one, had lacked the attention he needed to set him on a less destructive path. And Charlene and Patsy had blindly followed Ma's example.

I'd never wanted children. It used to embarrass me to admit it; after all, it wasn't a "natural attitude" for a woman. But then I'd connected with many other women who felt the same way and realized it didn't make us unwomanly or unfeeling or downright evil. It was mainly that we sensed we wouldn't be good parents, and that would be unfair to our offspring.

I love kids, young adults even more. And a good thing too, because I have all these young people—both related and not related—who flock around. They aren't mine, but in some ways they are, and I care for them as I would for my own. It's been a pleasure watching them grow and change, but without the ultimate responsibility for them.

8:20 p.m.

A car, gray, one of those nondescript models whose shape always makes me call them "sausage cars," pulled up at the corner of Moraga and stopped. A figure got out and moved into the dark to the west. Looked like a man, but I couldn't be sure.

Mick said, "I'll check it out."

"Stay out of the light. And be careful."

"Right."

I switched off the light above the rearview mirror so it wouldn't go on when he opened the door. He slid from the car and melded into the darkness. I sat, watching and waiting, drumming my fingers on the steering wheel, and thinking about that voice on the phone. It had sounded familiar, but I was certain I hadn't heard it recently. Not in connection with the Warrick case, anyhow.

It wasn't long before Mick slid back into the car. "Whoever he or she is, I can't locate them. To the right of the chapel there's a patch of open space with stained glass windows overlooking it. The back and left side are wooded. That's where I guess he is. We should call the cops—"

"Not yet." I opened my door.

Mick grabbed my arm. "Shar, let me go with you. It's too dangerous alone—" And then he saw the .357 Magnum I'd just removed from my purse.

"I'll be all right," I said. "Give me ten minutes. If I'm not back by then—"

"I'll come running."

I closed the door with just the slightest click and moved

slowly across the intersection. At this time of night, there was little traffic—none at present. It was cold, and fog misted the treetops. Eucalyptus, cypress, and pine trees—many more than a hundred years old—crowded in on my right; their combined pungent smells filled my nostrils. Although I was some distance from the Bay the wind was chill and briny. Again I heard the bellow of the foghorns. Lights winked here and there from what I knew were pale stucco houses with red-tiled roofs, but they were screened by the trees and dimmed by the mist.

In spite of my brave words to Mick and the comfort of the .357, experience had taught me that many of these nighttime meetings ended up in firefights and fatalities. I had no idea who this person was or why he had summoned me here.

At the other side of the road I paused, avoiding the lighted front of the chapel, and listened. Heard nothing.

Okay, which was the best approach? On the side with the open space and stained glass windows, I'd make an easy target. Of course, so would he. If I moved close to the shrubbery he might try to jump me. And he might be armed—a flashlight, a gun, God knew what else.

So confuse him.

I continued along the road to the left, moving away from the chapel lights' glow. After about a hundred yards, I found a break in the shrubbery and slipped through. The small sounds I made sounded glaringly loud to me. I stopped to listen, but heard nothing but the wind.

When I reached the back of the chapel, the terrain there wasn't as overgrown as I'd thought it would be. Cautiously I moved forward, slipping my flashlight from my left-hand pocket. Stiffened when a dark shape crouched beside the chapel wall materialized ahead of me.

My foot slipped on the needle-covered ground, and before I could surprise him, the noise alerted him. He whirled, straightened, and rushed at me. I had a swift impression of a Giants baseball cap, a beard, a blue-and-yellow athletic jacket, as I dodged to one side.

He staggered past me, then righted himself and came at me again. But he tripped over something and went down in a forward sprawl. By the time he pushed up, I had the flashlight as well as the .357 trained on him.

He was nobody I'd ever seen before.

He stumbled to his feet, shielding his eyes. Decided against another attack and tried to run away instead. He didn't get very far because in the darkness he missed seeing a cypress tree and plowed headlong into it. The sound of impact was like a melon splatting on pavement.

Silence. Then a whimpering sound, as if from a hurt cat or dog.

My flashlight beam found him again. He was lying on the ground, clutching his left arm; from the angle he held it at, it looked to be broken. His eyes squeezed shut again in the glare from the flash, then opened to slits.

"Who the hell are you?" I demanded.

"Me?" He coughed, panted. "I'm...nobody."

The voice was the same as the one I'd heard on the phone. I raised the gun. "*Who?*"

"You...wouldn't know the name."

"Try me."

No answer.

"You tried to attack me. Why?"

More silence, except for his heaving breath.

"*Why?*"

"I want my lawyer."

Jesus, I wasn't even a cop and he was already lawyering up!

10:44 p.m.

My assailant was Dixon Cooley, a not-very-bright minor league hoodlum from LA who had been wanted for aggravated assault since 2010. His identity and address were all he would give up to the cops, and his lawyer, Michael Falvey, a well-known defender of rich, guilty, and/or publicity-seeking clients, arrived at the Hall of Justice within an hour and went into conference with his client. I gave a brief statement and was told I could go home, provided I came in for a more complete statement in the morning.

Michael Falvey representing a small-time thug? That suggested Cooley was connected to someone with big bucks and a strong desire to remain anonymous. Was he supposed to kill me? Beat me up? Threaten and intimidate me? Could be any of the three; Cooley wasn't talking on advice of counsel. Since the Warrick case was the only one I was working at the time, it seemed likely there was a connection. But no one I'd contacted regarding the case really fit into the category of persons who hire professional muscle.

When the police finally let us go, an officer gave us a ride back to my car in the Presidio.

I asked Mick, "Are you staying at the Tower tonight?"

"No, my place. Alison needs space to sort things through." After a pause, he added, "I need space too."

"Then I'll just drop you off."

"I didn't mean space from you. I just need time to focus without everything hanging over my head."

"I get you."

"So come on—keep me company."

11:33 p.m.

Mick's studio, down the Embarcadero from the doomed Pier 24½, reminded me of the flight control center in an airport. Three thirty-plus-inch computer monitors were mounted on the walls; keyboards, modems, scanners, and shelves holding spare parts surrounded us. That was it, except for a blue futon on a sagging wooden frame, a chessboard with pieces halted in the middle of a game, a tiny kitchen, and an equally tiny bathroom. The place was immaculately tidy, which surprised me, given Mick's tendency to shed unnecessary clothing and leave it on the floor.

Still, it was no wonder he spent so much time at Alison's, I thought. For most of his life Mick had grown up in big, luxurious houses. But maybe this was his cocoon.

A cocoon, the place we can hide and be safe, is something we all wish for. Mine, in my childhood fantasies, was a deep pit full of warm fur pelts where friendly people had put me to help me escape from my enemies. I didn't know where the pit was, who the kind people were, or what kind of enemies I had, but the fantasy put me to sleep whenever I indulged in it.

I lounged on the futon, trying not to nod off. "You staying here tonight?" I asked him.

"Yeah."

He continued with his searches. "What're you looking for?" I asked.

"When I went to check out that guy's car at the Presidio, I snapped a photo of the license plates with my cell. The 'sausage car' was an Enterprise rental, to Cooley. But it wasn't the only vehicle at the scene that's related to your case. Remember the van parked on that same block?"

"Yes."

"It was registered to old RadioactiveMac."

Daniel Winters, the angry former client; he must've been the one who hired Cooley and Falvey. And he'd gone to the Presidio to watch his revenge exacted in person.

Just let him wait to see the revenge *I* planned to exact.

THURSDAY, JANUARY 12

3:11 a.m.

I woke myself by snorting like a pig. I'd fallen asleep on Mick's futon.

God, I thought, *I've probably drooled on his pillow.*

Mick wasn't there, but a note was posted on the screen of the largest of his monitors: "Gone home to talk with Alison. Here's a list of Amelia's friends who said she'd been afraid before she was killed." It was complete with home addresses and various contact information.

I squinted at the time on the screen.

After three a.m. Where did he get his energy?

I sat up, retrieved my cell from my bag, and almost called him. Stopped myself; this was a critical point in his relationship with Alison. They didn't need any interference.

I wanted to go home. I wanted to curl up in my own bed with my cats and await a call from Hy. But I didn't feel like driving across town to Church Street in the middle of the night.

I wrapped my arms around Mick's pillow—yep, I'd

drooled on it—and temporarily turned off my overactive mind.

6:08 a.m.

Why are those big eyes staring at me?

I must have been dreaming. No, I was half awake and the eyes were actually computer monitors—big ones. Of course—I'd fallen asleep at Mick's. For a moment I watched the screen savers: Alison smiling in front of a Christmas tree; Hy and me at Touchstone; a hideous, leering gorilla. I wondered what the gorilla signified, then decided I didn't really want to know.

Daylight. And Mick still wasn't back. It must've gone well with Alison. I wondered if I would become a great-aunt soon.

I went into the bathroom to clean up and straighten my slept-in clothes, but that didn't make me look much more presentable, and I had to go to the Hall of Justice to give a more complete statement on the assault upon me by Dixon Cooley.

Time to go home for a shower and a change of clothing before beginning my day.

9:05 a.m.

"Dixon Cooley won't talk about his attack on you," said Inspector Kay Singer of Robbery and Assault. "Thanks, or no thanks, to Iron Mike Falvey."

"I think it was a man named Daniel Winters who hired both of them. And I think Cooley or Winters was responsible for the elevator crash at my agency's building."

"The elevator crash? Oh, yeah, I read about that. What makes you think so?"

"Didn't you receive a report from one of my operatives about the presence of a vehicle at the Presidio scene registered to Winters?"

Singer shuffled through the file on her desk. "No...yes, here it is. Who's Winters?"

"A former client who tried to use me to cover up an insurance fraud. This wimp gets out of jail, sabotages my elevator. Posts a threat to me on a cold case site, and then hires a stupid thug to push me around. It's like kids squabbling on a playground."

"Squabbling kids don't carry knives—usually." She held up an evidence bag containing a wicked-looking hunting knife. "What did Winters hire you for?"

"He's an idiot archaeologist from UC–Berkeley who claimed his artifacts were stolen and tried to use me to verify his insurance claims were valid; I found out that he'd really sold the stuff. He did time, now he's out, and using his stupidity to the max."

"Well, we can't prove he had anything to do with the assault unless Cooley talks. And it doesn't look like he will. But we can nail him, at least. All we need is an additional statement from you after you've picked him out of a lineup."

Great, just great! The son of a bitch would legally get away with what he'd ordered done to me. But he wouldn't for long. He was on my shit list now, and somehow, someday he'd pay for it.

11:05 a.m.

The wheels grind slowly at the Hall of Justice. I was at a medium boil, having wasted my morning when I had more important concerns.

Finally the lineup got under way, and there was Cooley, looking like a depressed rat without a tail. I had to smile, because one of the officers I knew on Vice—really quite a handsome man—had volunteered for the event, and whatever he'd done to his hair and mustache had made him look even worse, like a rat that'd been dunked in Lysol.

I identified Cooley and left the Hall, headed for the office.

There was a message from Richard Gosling, Caro's therapist. I called but Gosling was with a patient. I considered the list that Mick had compiled of Amelia's friends, decided that I'd better show up in person to interview them, thus having the advantage of surprise on my side. If any of them had guilty knowledge of Amelia's death, they wouldn't have time to prepare a cover story.

Still nothing from Mick. I decided he and Alison had had enough time to work things through. But when I called his cell, he didn't answer. Well, he'd done this before, but it was a workday, and I was getting tired of reminding him of the agency rule about checking in. I ought to be more understanding, given his current situation. No, I ought to fire him. No, if I did, my sister Charlene would skin me alive—one of the hazards of having relatives work for you in this business.

My phone rang—Dr. Richard Gosling. His voice was low and pleasant, the sort that would inspire confidence in his patients. I explained who I was and what I was after, and there was a pause. Then he said, "You must understand, Ms. McCone, that doctor-patient confidentiality extends beyond the patient's death. Did Ms. Warrick give you written authorization to speak with me before her...untimely demise?"

"No, but I'd planned to ask for it."

"Then I'm sorry, but I can't help you."

"Her brother, Rob, is executor of her estate. Could he authorize it?"

"That's somewhat unorthodox."

"As I understand it, the executor is bound to act in the best interests of the estate. It would seem to me that determining who killed Ms. Warrick and why would certainly be of benefit."

"In what way?"

I dipped into my treasure chest of lawyer-speak, filled from years of keeping my ears opened at All Souls Legal Cooperative. "From what Rob's told me, while the will leaves substantial bequests to Ms. Warrick's sister and brother, it mainly benefits two organizations advocating gun control. There are certain pro-gun individuals and organizations that might seek to challenge it. Although the will is valid, anyone, as you probably know, can file a suit. If the judge assigned to the case is favorable to one side or the other—and face it, many of our judges, at all levels, are biased—it may either be tossed out as frivolous or tried in court. If it goes to trial, and even if the judgment goes against the contesting party, there are appeals and stalling tactics, which would indefinitely deprive the other beneficiaries of their bequests."

Another long pause. Then, "Ms. McCone, are you sure you're an investigator, not an attorney?"

"I've picked up enough information from an entire career of working with lawyers that I'm sure I could pass the state bar exam with a little coaching."

He chuckled. "Yes, I believe you could. Here's what I'll do: call the brother, and if he has no objection, I'll ask for written authorization to speak with you and schedule an appointment."

"Thank you, Dr. Gosling. How long will that take?"

His sigh said, *Don't you ever let up?* Aloud he said, "If all goes well, I can see you tomorrow afternoon at two."

Success! I told myself as I broke the connection. Then I reinforced it by calling Rob Warrick and warning him of Gosling's forthcoming request.

"No worries," he said. "I'll expedite it, deliver the authorization to him in person."

"How are you doing?"

"So-so." I could picture him waggling a hand from side to side. "I called the Pines in Santa Barbara to ask how Patty was doing. They said she had a 'little outburst' last night, but was now 'nicely sedated.' I know what her 'little outbursts' are like, and believe me, they're not pretty. And as for 'nicely sedated,' I'll bet they've given her such strong meds that she might as well be on another planet."

"Did she ever see Richard Gosling?"

"No. My parents were more concerned with her body than her mind. They sent her to a lot of fat farms, with no lasting results."

"Are they still in town?"

"Hell no. I'm amazed they even came to the service. Probably Ben had business here, so it was convenient. By now they're in Caracas or Tuscany, or wherever else they go."

"I'm surprised they can afford to travel so much. Caro said they were in tight straits because of the costs of her trial."

"That was just Caro-speak. No, it was a Caro-lie. Damn, there were so many of them. But I loved her in spite of them. I still do."

I liked this man: he was emotional, practical, and self-aware.

"Okay," I said, "I've taken up enough of your time. I'll keep you posted."

1:37 p.m.

"Those last couple of weeks, I couldn't believe what Amelia was telling me." Kimberly Smith, Amelia's friend, sat across from me in a coffee shop on busy Lombard Street. "I mean, a guy in a black cape following her—it was too Jack the Ripper."

"But she did seem genuinely afraid?"

"Yeah, that's the weird thing. She'd have you completely believing her, and later you'd think about it and go, *She's gotta be making this up.*"

I studied Kimberly. She was petite, blond, with an up-turned freckled nose. Currently unemployed and living with her parents on Cervantes Street, but "looking for something in a creative field." From her expensive wool coat and the Cervantes Street address, I knew her parents were well off and she could take her time looking.

"How long had you known Amelia?" I asked.

"Hmmm. We met at a party at a friend's house about a year before....Can't remember whose house—you know how people come and go in this city. Decided to go jogging the next day. We were both so hungover, we ended up at a bar in a Mexican restaurant. El Pico de Gallo, here on Lombard. Drank margaritas and told tales most of the afternoon."

"What kind of tales?"

"Just tales. You know how it is: boyfriends, movies you've seen, good restaurants, even books. After that, we planned to jog every Sunday—and sometimes we did— but we always went to Pico's."

"Did you jog the Sunday before she died?"

"Yeah. She mentioned being scared again, kept looking over her shoulder. Later, at Pico's, she insisted on taking a booth at the very rear."

"And that was your last contact with her?"

"It was." She looked down, fiddled with a silver bracelet on her right wrist. "You know, I've often thought that if I'd only taken her more seriously instead of getting hung up on the thing with the cape, she might not've been murdered."

"Even if you had, what could you have done? Someone was determined to kill her, and if it hadn't happened the way it did, they'd've probably changed their modus operandi and taken her out later."

"But why? Why would anybody want her dead? Not Caro Warrick. I knew and liked her. She was a good friend to Amelia. And Amelia—you couldn't find a nicer, more caring woman."

"'Why' is what I'm going to find out."

2:40 p.m.

Another friend of Amelia's, Sarah Katz, met me at a country-and-western bar on lower Russian Hill. She must've been a regular—several patrons and the bartender called out hellos to her—and an ardent fan, because her cowboy boots, jeans, Western jacket and hat spoke of Nashville. When she greeted me, her accent was pure Southern.

Now, there was a way of establishing rapport. "Country fan, are you?"

"Major."

"My brother-in-law's Ricky Savage."

"Oh my God. My *God!*"

"Actually he used to be my brother-in-law, but now he's married to my best friend, so I guess he's still related in an odd way."

"What's he like?"

"Pretty much like he is on stage—friendly, easygoing, unpretentious."

"I knew it. I just *knew* he would be."

"He's not performing as much as he used to—running Zenith Records and finding new talent takes up a lot of his time—but the next time he does a show in the Bay Area, I'm sure he'd be happy to put you and a friend on his guest list."

"You don't know what that would mean to me."

I've never understood our national obsession with celebrities. A pop star can overdose and it goes on the front page, but a physicist can win the Nobel Prize and the story is buried on page five. Of course, my attitude could stem from the fact that I've never known a Nobel winner, but have known my family's particular celebrity since he was dirt-poor and playing high school dances such as the one where he'd met Charlene.

"It's a done deal," I told her. "Now, let's talk about Amelia."

"God, I got so carried away—"

"That's okay. How long before Amelia's death had you known her?"

"Since college. We met in an English composition class. I stayed and got my BA. She left, but we still saw each other."

"How often?"

"A couple of times a month."

"What did you do together?"

"Had lunch, went to special exhibits at the museums if there were any good ones."

"You were both interested in art, then."

"Yes. I teach art at a small girls' school on the Peninsula. Amelia...well, she still was floundering to find something she really wanted to do. Those modeling jobs, they were ludicrous for someone of her talents."

"Talents, such as...?"

"She could've been a graphic designer, done something with her writing, or with photography. She could've gone to graduate school in any number of fields. But instead she did nothing but occasional photo shoots and hitting the club scene." Sarah paused. "The last time I saw her—three weeks before…you know—I came down on her pretty hard about her lack of initiative. We didn't part on the best of terms, and now I wish I'd kept my mouth shut."

"You'd've eventually patched it up."

"I know. But now we can't—not ever."

I have a number of similar regrets. All I could do was pat Sarah's hand.

4:29 p.m.

I hadn't been able to get hold of the third friend of Amelia's on my list, so I turned toward the RI building, thinking to check up on how things were going in our new space. But as I crossed Market Street, my phone rang: Mick.

"Where the hell have you been?" I demanded. "I know you and Alison needed to talk things out, but you've taken the whole day off. You have a job here, not a hobby, you know—"

"Stop!"

"It's inconsiderate. It's against agency policy. It's—"

"Just stop already! I've got a serious situation on my hands. Can you meet me at Jake Green's place in Atherton?"

"What're you doing there?"

"Please. Just come. I…need you."

The gravity in his voice damped my anger. "Sure."

"To get here you take 280 South till you hit—"

"I have the address and I'll use my GPS to find it."

"Okay. The house is set back and flanked by palms. Spanish-style, looks small, considering the price tag."

"I take it Green's not there."

"Just get down here—fast!"

5:17 p.m.

The afternoon light was fading when I located Green's house. It *did* look small, considering the size of the other properties I'd passed along the winding, tree-shaded street. I drove up a blacktop driveway into a circular parking area with a fountain in its center—water spraying from what looked like a trumpet vine flower into a simple marble basin. Mick's Harley was nowhere in sight.

Frowning, I got out of the car and followed a flagstone walk to the front door. Rang twice, but received no answer. There was another path along the left side of the house; when I started along it, Mick popped out from behind a yew tree, his finger to his lips.

"What the hell...?" I whispered.

He put his arm around my shoulders and led me to where the path opened into an enormous backyard with a sweeping green lawn, a detached four-car garage, flower beds alive with winter blooms, an Olympic-size pool, and what I assumed must be a pool house.

"There," he said, pointing to the pool.

I stepped forward, my breath catching as I saw a man floating facedown in a spot of pinkish-hued water. I recognized Jake Green by the perfectly round bald spot on the crown of his head. There was a raggedy, stained hole in his once-white shirt.

"Jesus," I said. Looked away, took a couple of breaths, then looked back. The shirt was not only bloodstained but had a dark smear around the bullet hole that looked as if it might be gunpowder residue. It would have washed away, if trapped air had not pushed the shirt above the water's surface.

"You call the police?" I asked Mick.

"No. I wanted you to see this first."

"Mick, somebody might've seen you come in here—"

"I parked my bike around the corner; there are a couple of others there that're probably snooting mine because it's not as classy. In case you didn't notice, these houses are set far apart and three of them are vacant and for sale: no prying eyes."

I studied Green's body again. "Shot in the back. Can't tell from here if it was point-blank or not. But judging from the dark stains on his shirt, the killer stood close."

"Somebody he knew?"

"Maybe."

"Pro hit?"

"Could be." I turned and surveyed the house. The French doors to the pool area were open.

Mick looked alarmed. "Shar, you're not—"

"Yes, I am. I want you to remove my car from the driveway. Take it down to the turnout near the freeway and walk back."

"This is not a good move."

"I'm sick of good moves. I'm sick of being the good kid on the block. I'm tired of rules."

"What the hell is the *matter* with you?"

"Maybe when you're my age and have my experience you'll understand. Maybe not. I'm not sure I really understand it myself yet."

"Give me a clue."

"Not now—just go!"

"I will, but don't you take a step inside until I get back."

5:40 p.m.

After the sound of my Z4 faded down the winding road, I stood next to the pool where Jake Green's body floated, the water occasionally stirred by the filtration mechanism. I knew speed was necessary here, but I felt sluggish, an aftereffect of the revelation of being sick and tired of being the good kid who followed the rules that I'd— clumsily—shared with Mick minutes before.

Something in me had snapped at the sight of Green's body, something that couldn't be pasted—or even Gorilla Glued—back together.

Hy had spoken to me of breaking points like this. When a violent event brought about a change in your emotional reactions and you were never again the person you had been before.

I was angry—but it was a cold anger. I didn't care that Jake Green was dead in his pool. If I'd had my .357 with me, I wouldn't have minded shooting him again—a symbolic remove-you-from-the-rest-of-humanity gesture. A gesture that once I would have considered barbaric.

Not any more.

Since I didn't have the gun, I went on to the more logical thing: a search of his house. Disobeying Mick's orders, I took out my flashlight and went inside.

The French doors led into a rec room: fireplace, pool table, old-fashioned jukebox, comfortable-looking furnishings. I scanned the walls beside the door for an alarm keypad, found one to the right that had been disarmed. There could be separate alarm systems on the other doors, but I'd deal with them later.

The room was a mess. Dirty glasses and plates sat on dust-covered surfaces. Newspapers, including last Sunday's *San Jose Mercury News*, from which the *Chron* had picked up the "Where Are They Now" story, were scattered about on the coffee table and the floor. One section was opened to a retrospective on Amelia Bettencourt's murder and Caro Warrick's acquittal that was similar to the one that had led me to Dave Walden.

I didn't subscribe to the *Mercury*, but I knew it to be a good paper. I scanned the piece, found it accurate, and also found a reference to Jake Green. He was described as an "entrepreneur dealing in international commodities exchanges."

Not a struggling travel agent?

What commodities? Corn? Wheat? Pork bellies?

And dealing with whom? China? African countries? South America?

Whatever the answer, Jake Green hadn't been pleased with the publicity: the page from the *Mercury* was crumpled and torn.

I checked the reporter's byline: Rebecca Regan. I didn't know her, but I hoped to shortly make her acquaintance.

6:20 p.m.

"Shar, come on out of there!" Mick, calling from outside by the pool again. "I told you to wait for me."

I went to the French doors and said, "A few more minutes."

He was standing a few feet away, his hands fisted. I couldn't see his expression in the shadows, but I imagined it was angry.

"How many more?" he asked.

"Ten, maybe fifteen."

"Look, we've got a dead guy in the pool and God knows who might show up—"

"Nobody's going to show up."

"How d'you know that?"

I didn't, exactly, but I sensed Jake Green was the kind of man who would invite few people into his home—and none who would drop in spontaneously.

When I didn't respond, Mick asked, "What about his security system?"

"I've spotted one keypad—for the French doors that're open. Now that you're here, you might as well look for junction boxes and wiring. Do what you can to disarm them."

"Right. But Shar—"

"Fifteen minutes, tops."

6:24 p.m.

What I'd seen in the rec room didn't reflect the rest of the house. The kitchen was equally messy, but the rooms behind it were strangely tidy, full of African tribal artifacts, some of them over eight feet tall. Rugs whose origin I couldn't begin to guess at hung on wires from the ceilings, creating a maze that was difficult to navigate. In one room was a shrine with a studio portrait of Amelia flanked with light bulbs that flickered to emulate candles.

So maybe he *had* really loved her, and not just for her money.

No telling what kind of man Jake Green had been. Complicated, I supposed, like so many people.

"Shar! I've done all I can with the alarm system. It's time to come out of there!"

"I haven't even gone upstairs yet."

The staircase was curved, without a landing, carpeted in blue. I climbed it to a short hallway. Bathroom: spacious, with a large shower that could be entered from either of the rooms that flanked it. Bedroom: neatly made up, no sign of recent occupancy. Another bedroom: rumpled bedclothes, clothing tossed around indiscriminately, but no signs of violence.

Mindful of Mick's anxiety, I swiftly but carefully went through the closets and drawers. Jake Green had possessed an uncommon number of shoes and suits, dress and casual shirts. Coins and a thick wad of bills secured by a money clip lay on the dresser. The clip was inscribed with Green's initials. There was a wallet: driver's license, ATM card, an unusual number of credit cards—two or three each from Visa, MasterCard, American Express, Discover, Capital One.

A lacquered red-and-black box sat beside the wallet; it was crammed with costly-looking chains and rings.

In the bathroom I found no prescription medicines and no over-the-counter drugs except aspirin. I also learned that he used Crest toothpaste, Dial soap, and Rogaine—apparently he hadn't been one of the people for whom the hair loss remedy worked.

I hurried back downstairs in time to hear Mick's muted voice say, "Shar—come here!"

"Where?"

"Stairway off this little telephone nook by the kitchen."

I'd noted the nook before.

"You won't believe this!" he added.

"I'm coming!"

The stairs were old and worn, the passage of many feet having gouged deep but smooth depressions. I put my hand on the railing, then removed it, afraid it would give. Mick had turned the lights on in the basement, and at first I saw only an old-fashioned laundry room with a wringer washing machine and an ironing mangle in one corner; then he gestured through a door to his left.

Crates. Open crates full of guns. And not just any kind of guns: these were weapons of war.

Enough of them to supply a small army.

Some I recognized because RI possessed them in its not-inconsiderable arsenal: AK-47s, AR-15s, Heckler & Koch 416s.

Others were unfamiliar, but all were black and ugly, nesting in their soft pink packing material that incongruously reminded me of cotton candy.

The damage these could do, the lives that could be lost.

Up to now I'd considered my .38 and .357 dangerous

weapons, but their capacity paled in comparison to the crated firepower.

Mick was inspecting rows of stacked boxes. "Lots of ammo here too."

I said, "So Green wasn't just laundering money for other people; he was earning a lot of it by trading in arms."

"Nice little cottage industry."

"Seems to me he was careless, leaving all this in an unlocked room."

"There's an alarm on this door, but I got past it."

"How?"

He held up something that looked like a flash drive for a computer. "Decoding device. Something I whipped up in my spare time."

Sometimes he purely amazed me.

"So what now?" he asked.

"This case has gotten entirely too big for us. It's time to bring in the police—the FBI and ATF, too."

I started for the stairs, taking out my cell; Mick was close behind. But just as I put my foot on the first step, sounds from above froze me in place.

Somebody else was in the house.

Mick heard them too. "What do we do now?" he whispered.

"Nothing yet. Until we know who they are, we don't want to reveal ourselves."

The footsteps were louder overhead now—more than one person coming through the front door.

I grabbed Mick's arm, pulled him back into the laundry room. "Over here!"

The mangle was a huge contraption left over from the

days when proper housewives—or more likely their servants—wouldn't dream of making up a bed with sheets that hadn't been ironed. Supported on thick legs at either end, it was pulled away from the wall just far enough that Mick and I could slip behind either leg. I scraped my back on the rough wall, glanced at Mick and saw him grimace as he did the same.

Somebody yelled, "Jesus Christ, look out there!" and I knew they'd sighted Green's body.

I whispered to Mick, "Did you disarm the front door?"

"No. It's not linked with the others."

"So whoever it is has a key and the code."

Now the intruders were on the stairs. Two of them, I thought, but I didn't dare look to be sure. A man's voice said, "This is where he stores the stuff," and they went into the adjoining room.

Mick moved his head, indicating we should try to escape while they were inside.

I shook mine firmly, rolled my eyes toward the ceiling. Someone was still walking around upstairs.

Voices came from the room where the arms were stored, but I couldn't make out the words. After a short while they became clearer.

A hoarse-sounding man said, "But why was that alarm off and the door open? And if it's not in there, where did he put it?"

"Maybe whoever shot him got the code out of him first," his companion suggested.

"Maybe. Better hope not."

A third man's steps came down the stairs. "Doesn't look like anybody's gone through the rest of the house. Whoever blew Green away either got what he wanted down here or took off when we arrived."

"It's not in there with the guns."

"Did you look for it? *Really* look?"

"Whaddaya think we are, imbeciles?"

Long silence. Then all three laughed with varying degrees of nervousness.

"Ah, shit," the hoarse-voiced man said, "let's get outta here before somebody else shows up."

"Amen to that, brother."

7:43 p.m.

Mick and I waited fifteen minutes after they were gone before we wormed our way out of our hiding place and stretched the kinks from our cramped bodies.

"I'm getting too old for this sort of thing," I said.

"Me too, or at least I'd like to," he replied. "What now? Search the house for whatever they wanted?"

"They knew what it was and didn't find it. What chance does that give us?"

"Virtually none."

"Okay, now we'll turn this over to the cops and the feds."

9:58 p.m.

I leaned my forehead against my left hand, eyes burning from the light of the overhead fluorescent bulbs of an interview room at the Atherton Police Department. So far I'd spoken with officials of the FBI, the ATF, and other interested agencies; been given four cups of bad coffee and a turkey sandwich with a suspiciously rancid smell; and phoned my criminal defense attorney, Glenn Solomon, who was now on his way down the Peninsula. I'd asked about Mick, but had been told nothing; I'd volunteered to have my case files messengered down from my office and been told that wasn't necessary; and I'd been subjected to various scathing comments—from both men and women—about my professional life and style.

"Don't respect the rules much, do you, McCone?"

Nope, not when they're the wrong rules.

"Think you can get involved in any kind of mess and walk away unscathed."

Not when you've been beaten up, stabbed, shot in the ass, and shot in the head, and you've ended up in a coma for over two weeks.

"Shield your clients whether they're guilty or not, don't you?"

I've turned in every guilty client I've ever had.

"Trade on the fact you're a woman, I've heard."

Come on, this is the twenty-first century. I trade on the fact that I'm damn good at what I do.

"That husband of yours, he's a loose cannon. Doesn't play by the rules either."

Then why have your agencies relied on him time and time again?

"That attorney who killed himself last year—wasn't that your fault?"

No, it was his, because he was a child molester.

"That crazy druggie brother of yours who's locked up in an institution—was he a molester too?"

Darcy. My half brother whose bad genes came from a heroic, idealistic, charismatic, but ultimately unstable leader of the American Indian Movement. Darcy, who was working hard to overcome his inherited problems...

The latter comment tipped the scales. Up till then I'd conducted myself in a reasonably calm and courteous manner. But now...

"I'm not listening to any more of your shit," I said evenly. "I'm the party who offered her assistance to you, and for some reason—probably because I do my job better than any of you do yours—you're harassing me. I'm leaving now, and I'm taking my nephew with me."

"You can't—" one of the suits began.

"Yes, I can, unless you decide to charge both of us. And just what would you charge us with?"

One of them began, "Obstruction—" and then was shut up by a warning look from a colleague.

"I'll be going now," I told them, "and I'll expect to meet Mr. Savage on the front steps. My attorney, Glenn Solomon, is waiting there with selected members of the press." Even though he hadn't said anything about summoning the press when I talked with him, I knew that was what he'd done.

The atmosphere in the room became flat and subdued. There were a few coughs and a rustling of folders in the room. They knew very well what the consequences of this rude interrogation would be.

10:23 p.m.

Flashlights popped and video cams and microphones were pushed into my face. I kept saying, "No comment, no comment," as Glenn ushered Mick and me to the waiting limo.

He'd done his usual Solomon-style thing, but I wasn't at all sure I appreciated it. It would only strain my relations with the various law-enforcement agencies and make me more visible in a profession where anonymity is an asset.

As we got settled and the limo took off, I said, "All I tried to do was share what I knew with the cops and the feds. They jumped all over me."

Glenn put a big arm around my shoulders. "State of the world these days, my friend. We're more paranoid than we have been since the humanoids were battling the Neanderthals."

"Wonderful," I said. "This limo wouldn't happen to have a bar, by any chance?"

Glenn laughed, opened the bar built into the back of the driver's seat, and poured three large portions of something that looked dark and strong, handing one to me and one to Mick, and keeping the third for himself.

"As I see it," he said, "they didn't want to believe your story that something other than those stockpiled weapons was the reason Jake Green was murdered, so they focused on you and Mick and your presence on the property."

"And how long will it take for them to leave Mick and me alone and do their jobs?"

"As long as it takes for the media to have its way with

them, and for me to call them to the attention of my intel-ligent—and I use that word loosely—contacts in DC."

"In the meantime, what do I do?"

"Business as usual, my friend. But I would advise cau-tion. *Extreme* caution, until this case is over with."

I looked at Mick. "You hear that? Extreme caution."

"Yes, ma'am."

"That means for both you and Alison."

"What about Alison?" His tone was curiously blank.

"You saw her and talked things over, right?"

"She talked, I didn't."

"And?"

"Look, today's been all I can take for now. Just let it be, and take me back to my condo."

"For tonight I'll let it be, but you're coming to my house."

FRIDAY, JANUARY 13

*F*riday the thirteenth. *Thank God I'm not supersti-
tious.*

That was my first thought upon waking early; then I lay
in bed thinking about all that had happened before and
after Caro Warrick had hired me.

Amelia Bettencourt, murder victim. Jake Green, now
also a victim but previously Caro's and then Bettencourt's
boyfriend and, more recently, a money launderer and
dealer in illegal firearms. Caro, acquitted of the murder
of her friend, but intent on having the case reinvestigated
in the hope, I suspected, of finding out who really killed
Amelia. Caro, fatally injured outside my home while attempting to bring me documents she'd removed from her
self-storage unit. The dysfunctional Warrick family...I'd
tended to discount them because my own family was so
out of whack, but maybe I should look at them more seriously.

Ben and Betsy: experts in denial. Acting as if their son
Rob hadn't accidentally shot his baby sister with a loaded
gun his father had carelessly left in an accessible place.

Acting as if Marissa had never existed. Rob, they claimed, hadn't been shattered by the event, nor had Patty or Caro. Caro had had a bit of trouble when her best friend was killed, but that was over. And Ben and Betsy were now free to travel the world and meet exciting people.

Rob had received no significant help from his parents after he killed Marissa, nor had Patty. And Caro...? She had been the most vulnerable of them all.

A sad, grotesque family drama, but what did it have to do with arms smuggling and money laundering? If anything?

Okay, go on—to Dave and Kayla Walden. Dave had been mentioned in the retrospective about Caro's trial. Why? I'd have to ask the reporter who had written the piece. Caro had twice called the Waldens' home, but to me they had denied knowing her. They were outgoing with visitors to their winery but remote from their neighbors in a valley where fellow residents were usually close. Russ Hewette was a good example of that: they bought his grapes, but he'd had no direct contact with them for at least two and a half years. Had they a connection with the rest of the Warrick family? Jake Green? The Bettencourts?

The Bettencourts. Now, there was an angle I hadn't explored. Amelia's mother, Iris, was dead, but her father, James, lived down in Monterey County. If I could reach him later this morning, and he agreed to see me, I could be there in a couple of hours.

I told myself to go back to sleep for a while, but my thoughts and suppositions went on and on....

9:54 a.m.

Mick was gone when I went to look for him. Another elusive exit from my house by one of the Savage offspring. Last night he'd refused to talk about his meeting with Alison, and now he was avoiding me. That was okay; I'd wring the story out of him sooner or later. Right now I needed to get on with my investigation.

I was soon on the road to James Bettencourt's home in Pacific Grove, the top down on the BMW, the wind whipping my hair around and slowly sweeping away the sluggishness I'd felt upon awakening. Amelia's father had been gracious when I called and seemed eager to talk with me. I took the 280 freeway, cut across on the connector to Highway 17, then dropped down to Santa Cruz and followed the coastal route through Monterey to Pacific Grove.

As I drove down Lighthouse Avenue, I remembered the man I'd once thought to be my birth father, Austin DeCarlo. My connection with him had proved to be false, but for a while we'd bonded. Then I'd discovered he'd killed his own father—because of circumstances connected with my birth—and I had decided, out of compassion for Austin, to let the truth remain dormant. Last year Austin had died of a massive heart attack and, because there was no one else, had left the bulk of his estate to me—as well as the responsibility of having him cremated and his ashes scattered over Monterey Bay. I'd sold his house on the hill above Lighthouse Avenue and donated the proceeds to the Monterey Bay Aquarium. They'd named a sea otter in his honor.

It wasn't a responsibility I'd wanted, but it had been his way to express his gratitude.

I've always found Pacific Grove a charming place. The pace of life seems slower there, the close proximity of the Bay refreshing. A few streets of shops and restaurants, narrow lanes, houses perched on the hillside. One of my favorite writers, John Steinbeck, had lived there, and his descriptions of the gulls soaring over the sea and the thunder of waves on the offshore rocks are as fresh today as they were sixty-some years ago.

The directions that James Bettencourt had provided me led me up to a point much higher on the hill than Austin's former house. As I climbed, the view of the Bay became more and more spectacular. As a native Californian I'm familiar with the coast, but the variety of its more than seven hundred miles continues to amaze me. In San Diego, where I was born and raised, the beaches are very much like those pictured in the beach-blanket movies of the fifties and sixties. It's the same in the suburbs of LA and up to Santa Barbara. Farther north you've got more twists and turns in the road, steeper cliffs. When you get to Big Sur, you need to watch out for sleeper waves and landslides. The coast gentles at San Francisco, but once you reach the mouth of the Russian River at Jenner, whitecaps predominate. The road turns inland on a steep grade for miles, then emerges on a sheer cliff face that can be harrowing even to the most experienced driver. Heavily forested land and large, barren-looking ranches alternate. Finally the small town of Gualala—population some 900—slips by; later Point Arena—half Gualala's size—and a few other hamlets interspersed among the redwood, cypress, and oak trees.

And then there's our cove at Touchstone.

It's protected on three sides by cliffs, but the water conceals hazards: rugged rocks, kelp beds, and an ever-changing topography as the earth's tectonic plates shift and the tides erode. Some days the waves are placid, even at high tide; some days they roar and thrust upward, trying to reclaim the land. In a vicious winter storm I've seen logs four times the size of your average utility pole thrown three-quarters up the side of our cliffs.

The rest of the California coastline and up into Oregon and Washington is much the same: placid beaches, huge sea stacks, scalloped coves. And above all, it is as unpredictable as most of the people who live along it.

11:05 a.m.

James Bettencourt was slender—too thin, really—with thick gray hair and a face whose lines told of his grief and sorrow. He welcomed me into his attractive brown-shingled home, to a living room with a wall of glass overlooking the town, bay, and sea. He urged a glass of wine upon me, which I accepted in spite of the earliness of the hour, because I sensed he badly needed both a drink and someone to drink with. We settled on opposite ends of a sofa, looking out at a glorious day.

Bettencourt said, "I'm so glad someone's finally taking a serious interest in my Amelia's death."

"No one has before?"

"The police in San Francisco were too quick to jump on a suspect. They made ridiculous assumptions. There is no way that Caro Warrick would have killed my daughter. After her acquittal they put the case on the back burner, still claiming Caro did it and there had been a miscarriage of justice. They've never looked at it again, as far as I know. And now Caro's gone."

"You seem to have been very fond of Caro."

"Both my wife and I were, yes. She was a stabilizing influence on Amelia. I thought of her as holding fast to the string of a kite as it was buffeted by strong winds."

"And those strong winds were...?"

He rubbed at his tired eyes. "Amelia was always a problem child. As soon as she was put in her crib, she'd scream until one of us picked her up and rocked her; when she went to sleep and we put her down, the screaming would start all over again. By the time she got over that, she'd become very aggressive toward the other children in the neighborhood—pulling hair, kicking, biting. Next thing we knew she was destroying other children's toys at preschool. Of course, they told us she must leave.

"After that there were a few years of what my wife and I called the 'quiet time,' but next she was caught shoplifting and keying expensive vehicles."

"How old was she then?"

"Eleven."

"And what did you do about it?"

"Sent her off to a school for problem children. They, ah, returned her to us after she smashed a mirror and cut her wrists. The cuts, they said, weren't life-threatening, but a cry for help they weren't equipped to give."

"And then?"

"She seemed to settle down again. We took her to a

good therapist, enrolled her in a private school. She got decent grades, made friends, Caro Warrick being the closest. They did homework together, spent weekends at each other's houses. Amelia had poor grades; if she had gotten into college, she wouldn't have done well. Caro was very bright, but disorganized. She tried City College, but that didn't work out. So both girls took nothing jobs in the city—low-level temp work, some modeling—and played around in the evenings. Caro did all right, but Amelia didn't have good judgment about boys."

"In particular, Jake Green."

He nodded somberly. "And now he's dead too."

"Mr. Bettencourt, can you think of any connection between the murders of your daughter, Caro Warrick, and Jake Green?"

After a few seconds of reflection he replied, "No, I can't think of a single one. Do you think they're connected?"

"Yes," I said. "Somehow, some way."

"I wonder…"

"What?"

"On her last visit home, Amelia hinted to my wife and me that she was seeing someone other than Green. Someone who, if things worked out, would provide her with a wonderful life."

"Those were her exact words?"

"I'm not sure. Maybe there was something about a place, too. Frankly, I didn't take it all that seriously. My daughter spent much of her life wrapped in daydreams."

3:43 p.m.

I'd stayed too long in Pacific Grove to make my two o'clock appointment with Richard Gosling, Caro's therapist, so I called him and he agreed to reschedule for four. I stopped for lunch at a favorite restaurant on the water in Monterey—monster artichoke stuffed with marinated shrimp—and then got caught in a traffic jam in Santa Cruz. The news reports were saying that people were moving out of our overtaxed and underemployed state in droves, but you couldn't prove it by my experience.

Gosling's office was in the 450 Sutter Street building—a twenty-six-story Art Deco creation much favored by doctors, dentists, and other professionals. I rode the elevator to the nineteenth floor and located his suite, waited five minutes—too bad; his magazines were a cut above most found in anterooms—and was ushered by his receptionist to the inner sanctum.

At first glance Gosling looked old and frail, gray hair a wild cloud around his head, but his strong handshake conflicted with my impression.

He seated me, offered coffee, and waited intently, studying me with soft brown eyes. I was glad I wasn't one of his patients: those eyes would see my pretenses and all the lies I'd told myself.

He said, "As I told you in our phone conversation, this situation is unorthodox. However, Rob Warrick has delivered his authorization as executor of his sister's estate for me to speak with you. In fact, he was quite insistent that I do. So you may ask your questions."

"Dr. Gosling," I said, "how long was Caro Warrick a patient of yours?"

"Only for a few months after she was acquitted of her friend's murder."

"She sought you out because…?"

"Actually it was her brother Rob who sought me out. He practically had to drag her to her sessions."

"So you'd say she was a hostile patient?"

"Initially, yes. During our first session she didn't speak. The second session, she screamed and cursed at me, her family, and most of the people she'd ever known. It was a catharsis. Afterward she was docile, but she kept parroting the story she'd told at her trial."

"You say 'story.' I take it you didn't believe her."

"I believed that she'd been in Amelia Bettencourt's apartment that night. I believe she saw something terrible there. But do I believe she killed her friend? No, I don't."

"Did she ever confide anything to you that didn't come out at the trial?"

He considered. "Her parents both had numerous affairs. One of her mother's boyfriends tried to molest her, but her brother stopped him. I can't—oh, yes: Amelia was having an affair with an unnamed married man before she died."

"Unnamed?"

"Caro didn't know who he was, but she had some letters from Amelia about him. She said it sounded serious."

Letters: could they have been among the documents Caro was trying to deliver to me when she was bludgeoned to death?

"Is there anything else you remember?"

Gosling was silent for a moment, then shook his head. "If I recall anything more, I'll be sure to contact you. Caro was dear to me in a way most patients aren't."

"Why?"

"Because after all she went through, she was still an innocent; she still believed that life and people could be good."

"Do you believe that, Dr. Gosling?"

"I'm sorry to say I don't. You?"

"Occasionally. Only occasionally."

When I left 450 Sutter I first headed toward Pier 24½, then toward the blue building on Sly Lane, before I flashed on the new offices in the RI building.

McCone, are you losing it?

Something's out of whack, but it's not my mind. I'm simply a creature of habit.

I'd had similar distracted feelings time and time before. A fact was trying to wriggle its way out of the recesses of my consciousness, and I didn't dare grope for it. It would come eventually, and in the meantime I'd just have to put up with the abstraction and irritation.

6:37 p.m.

I sat at my desk, trying to catch up on the day's paperwork. Julia had successfully closed two cases; after editing her reports I sent them off to the clients, along with invoices. There were long e-mails in my inbox from a number of people, none of them in immediate need of a reply. Why, I wondered, did correspondents have to go on as if they were writing a segment of *War and Peace*? Wasn't e-mail supposed to be a brief and speedy form of communication?

Before I could get to my phone messages, the damned thing rang. I was tempted to let the call go to the machine, but picked up at the last minute.

"Ms. McCone?" a woman's voice said. "This is Nina Weatherford."

Who? Oh, yes, Jethro Weatherford's daughter. "Ms. Weatherford, my condolences again—"

"I'm on the way to Sonoma County to make arrangements for my father's burial, but decided to spend the night in the city. Since you were the one who last saw him, I'd like to talk with you, if you're willing."

"Of course. Where are you staying?"

"Hotel Vitale."

One of the Embarcadero area's better lodging places. "I can meet you in the lounge in, say, half an hour."

"Thank you, Ms. McCone."

7:07 p.m.

The Americano Restaurant and Bar at Hotel Vitale was warm and comfortable, with big plush chairs and leather banquettes, excellent city views, and soft-colored pine flooring.

Nina Weatherford had told me she would be wearing a black pantsuit with turquoise-and-silver earrings. I spotted her immediately on one of the banquettes, nervously toying with the stem of a wineglass.

She recognized me, had probably looked me up on Google. "Ms. McCone, thank you for coming."

I sat in the chair opposite hers. "It's good to meet you."

A waitperson came; I ordered a glass of pinot grigio.

Weatherford said, "Tell me what you know about my father's last hours."

"We'd talked for a while at the Jimtown Store, and he went back home to locate something for me. By the time I got there, he was dead."

"Did he suffer much?"

"I think death was instantaneous."

"Thank God." She took a large swallow of her wine. "Jethro—I thought he'd live forever when I was a kid. After I learned such things don't happen, I figured he'd be there for me all my life."

"But you'd been out of touch."

"Yes. My work keeps me in LA. I begged him to move down there so I could take care of him, but he wouldn't leave the valley. He was angry with me for not coming back. I tried to bridge the gap, but, well, he was a stubborn man. How did he seem before the end?"

"Pretty happy. Of course, the alcohol encouraged that."

"Yeah, Jethro was always fond of the sauce. But he was an amiable, gentle drunk."

"So you're planning services?"

"Well, I don't know how many people would attend. Daddy was pretty much a hermit since my mother died twenty years ago. I think a quiet, private burial will suffice."

"Where will that be?"

"On his little quarter acre. He never wanted to be anyplace else... Well," she added with a rueful smile, "maybe the Jimtown Store."

"That quarter acre of his—someone described it to me as worthless."

"Actually, it's pretty good land. Daddy just didn't want to work it. Didn't want to work at all."

"The Waldens—the new neighbors with the winery—claimed a corner of his land was theirs, but were proved wrong in court."

"Yes, he told me about that in one of our infrequent phone conversations."

"This was a couple of years ago, right?"

"Right. I wanted to refer him to a good lawyer I know here in the city, but as usual he got his back up and used somebody from up there."

"Do you remember which corner was in dispute?"

"Yes, I do."

I gave her a pen and she drew a map on a cocktail napkin. "This," she said, making an x, "is where the drainage tunnel from the Godden—now Walden—vineyards ends."

"Show me where it goes on the Walden property."

She drew a line between one of the Waldens' fields and the corner. "I used to creep around in there when I was a kid. Scared the hell out of Jethro by poking my head out of his end of it."

Now what could be so important about a drainage tunnel?

10:10 p.m.

Mick finally contacted me at home.

Irritably I asked him, "Where the hell have you been now?"

"Well, I emailed that *San Jose Mercury* writer, Rebecca Regan. The one who did that story on where are they now, and she asked me to come down for a breakfast meeting."

"Which lasted until well after dinner time?"

"Don't get sarcastic with me. I found out some good stuff."

"Such as?"

"Caro never bought the Glock the gun dealer testified she had—that's why it didn't show up in state records."

"They weren't expunged?"

"Never existed."

"So the dealer, Levinson, lied."

"It would appear so."

"Why didn't Regan come out with that fact at the time of the trial?"

He laughed. "Because she was in college back East then. She only became aware of the case when she was assigned that piece on the principals' whereabouts. But she got fascinated and dug deeper."

"So whose weapon was it?"

"I've tried to access the information, but had no luck."

"Try harder."

"I intend to."

"Did Regan tell you why Dave Walden was included in the piece?"

"His name came up in an old article and an interview

with Jake Green. He said she should talk with Walden, but she couldn't reach him and was on a tight deadline."

And, conveniently, Jake Green was dead.

"About this Rebecca Regan...?"

"Okay, okay. We talked a long time over breakfast. So then we went back to the Merc's offices and looked through her notes. It was late by the time we finished, so I took her out to lunch."

"And dinner?"

"I *like* her, Shar. She's easy to talk with, and there's not all this baggage that I have with Alison getting in the way."

"Baggage, such as a possible pregnancy?"

"Don't get on my case. Please. Not now."

"Okay, I'm sorry."

"It's not like I'm going to run off on Alison with a woman I've met once."

"And don't get defensive with me. Please."

"Okay. I'll call you when I've got more information."

"Mick? I love you."

"Me too, you."

I turned off my phone, gathered the cats, and went to bed.

SATURDAY, JANUARY 14

4:45 a.m.

I *was drifting on the waves, rising, falling, plunging. The*
sensation was pleasant, soothing me, but I warned my-
self not to go to sleep. I could drown.…

But these waves, they weren't water. Something softer,
like air.

The plane. I was in the plane—not the new one, but our
old Citabria, Seven-Seven-Two-Eight-Niner.

I wanted to slow down to enjoy the feeling a while longer,
but when I reached for the throttle, it wasn't there. I went to
pull back on the yoke, but it wasn't there either.

I spread my arms out, realized I wasn't in the plane at all.
Instead, I was free-falling.

I looked up for my parachute. It wasn't there either. Pan-
icked, I looked down at the ground. Nothing. All I could see
was a swirling grayness. It came at me and its fumes en-
veloped me and I took in a choking breath.

Smoke!

I woke quickly, sitting up in bed. Definite smell of
smoke; I hadn't been dreaming it. On Hy's pillow the cats
sat rigid, sniffing the air, their eyes wide and afraid.

Fire!

Where was it? Outside? In the house? Why hadn't the alarms gone off?

I scrambled out of bed and ran toward the sliding glass door. Next to it smoke billowed down the spiral staircase. I stared at the swirling gray in disbelief, and then my reflexes kicked in; my first thought was to grab the cats. I got hold of Alex, but Jessie darted under the bed.

"Damn useless animal!" I shouted at her as I tossed Alex out the door into the backyard.

The smoke was thickening enough to start me coughing. I stumbled around the bedroom, disoriented, trying to locate one of the light switches. When I found one, nothing happened—the power had gone out. Damn! Why had I bought plug-in detectors instead of the battery-operated kind?

Flattening on the floor beside the bed, I felt around for Jessie. She had backed into the far corner, and when I touched her she shrank out of my reach. I ducked my head lower and inched toward her, feeling the bedsprings rake at my scalp. When I was almost to her, she ran out from under the bed and straight through the door into the backyard.

Cursing the feline population in general, I dragged myself out and ran across the room too. As I passed the spiral staircase, what I saw made me cringe—at its top was a wall of flame: red and yellow and gold, tinged with green and black soot; angry, licking up toward the roof.

Phone!

The one down here was cordless, wouldn't work without electricity.

Cell!

Upstairs in my bag that I'd left on the kitchen table.

In the distance I heard sirens. Somebody had seen the smoke or the flames, called in an alarm.

Don't stand here like an idiot, McCone—get yourself out!

But I'm naked—

Stupid thing to think of in a life-threatening situation, but still I took the time to feel around for something to cover myself with. An old sweatshirt of Hy's hung on one of the chairs; I grabbed it, pulled it over my head as I plunged through the door.

The gravel under the upper deck lacerated my feet as I sprinted for the grass. Above, the deck railing collapsed, spewing sparks and burning fragments: one of the flaming posts fell directly on my shoulder, singeing my hair and setting my sleeve on fire.

I managed to slap out some of the flames, then threw myself down on the grass and rolled around till they were all out. My arm tingled, but it didn't feel badly burned. Finally, coughing and gasping, my heart pounding, I lay on my back, staring up at the smoke-palled sky.

Fire engines were out front now, men and women milling around and shouting. Jets of water spurted onto the roof and cascaded down the sides of the house. The engines' pulsing lights formed a lurid background to the flames.

Booted feet thundered on the walk to the side of the house. A male voice called, "Anybody here?"

"Yes," I said.

"You injured?"

I tried to sit up, then settled for a weak, "I'm okay," ignoring the increasing pain in my arm.

"You the owner?"

"Yes."

"Everybody else get out?"

"Yes."

"Okay, look, I'm gonna move you back toward the fence line. This is a bad one, and when the house collapses, we don't want you hurt." He picked me up as if I were a feather pillow and deposited me on the grass under the pines that grew there.

"Are the neighboring houses going to be okay?" I asked him.

"Looks like it. Everybody's outside and they're helping us by wetting down their roofs and walls."

"Thank God!"

From the front of my house there was a thunderous explosion; even from where I was I could feel its heat. Somebody yelled, "Watch out!" and there was a jarring crash that fouled the air with more smoke and sparks. Then the deck gave what I could only define as a sigh and crumbled.

I could do nothing but lie watching a vital part of my life burn to the ground.

The firemen did what they could, but they'd gotten there too late. When they finally had the blaze under control, the roof was gone and the rest of the house leaned in on itself. One upstairs wall groaned and collapsed into what had used to be the kitchen.

I closed my eyes and wept like a baby.

I had loved this house, had bought it when it was a decrepit wreck left over from the post–1906 quake era and made it a home. An earthquake house it was called by historians and architects, one of those small structures that had been put up here, in what was at that time the far reaches of the city, for the quake's survivors.

The previous owners hadn't tended to it in decades. Ceilings had caved in; floors were rotting; the toilet was in a cold cubicle on the back porch and didn't work all that well anyway. Refrigerator and stove: shot to hell. Tub and shower: not functional. But I've always been one to see potential in places, and over the years I'd made it a lovely place to live.

As much as I also loved Touchstone and the ranch in the high desert, this house was the first I'd ever owned, and the memories associated with it were precious.

"Shar? Thank God, Shar!"

The voice belonged to Michelle Curley, one of the young women from next door.

"Chelle," I said dully as she gathered me into her arms.

"We were so afraid!" she sobbed. "Mom saw the fire and called it in. Then she tried to call you, but she couldn't get through. And then the firefighters wouldn't let me past the barricades to look for you, so I came over the fence from our backyard. Are you okay?"

"I'm alive."

"Hurt?"

"Not much, physically. I'll have to get a haircut, though." I showed her the singed side of my head and laughed, trying to make a joke of it.

"Stop clowning around! You've got to be hurting bad inside. This house, all your stuff…"

"It can be replaced."

"You don't have to act brave in front of me," she said. "I've seen you brave before. But this…"

"Oh, shit." I started to cry again.

"Where's Hy?"

"Africa, somewhere."

"How do we get hold of him?"

"I don't know. I've told you about RI—they've got that damn need-to-know policy."

"Well, he needs to know. You want to go to emergency? Get checked out?"

"Chelle, I've had enough of hospitals to last the rest of my life."

"Then come home with me. Mom can put ointment on your burns, and I can make you soup. Then you can take one of Mom's pills and sleep."

"No sleeping pills. I've got to track down Hy. RI's staff is going to qualify this as a need-to-know situation. They'll damned well put me in touch with him."

Suddenly Chelle frowned. "The cats…?"

"Are outside, probably went over the back fence."

"I'll find them for you."

I stood up. The pain from the gravel lacerations was sharp. As we went down the walkway beside the ruins of my house I turned my head away. On the street I saw that both entrances to my short block of Church were cordoned off. The pavement was wet and glistening in the lights from the fire trucks, and the firemen were clearing up their equipment. Neighbors in bathrobes milled about; a few patted me sympathetically as Chelle and I moved toward a captain.

"You the owner?"

"Yes. Sharon McCone."

He told me his name was McCullough. "You're not injured?"

"No, I'm okay."

"Any idea of how this happened?"

"No. I had the furnace cleaned last fall, the ducts too. The hot water heater was new. The house was fully rewired a couple of years ago when we put on an addition. We don't store flammable substances in the garage."

The garage. My car. Oh, shit.

And then I thought of everything else I'd loved and lost: photographs; my old Nikkormat camera; quilts made especially for me by my sister Patsy; a steamer trunk that had been in my family forever. My grandmother's garnet earrings that I wore only on special occasions were in a US Navy ammo box anchored to the floor in the upstairs bathroom. My fish were by now boiled in their aquarium.

McCullough looked away, understanding what I was going through. A sudden wind brought whiffs of oily smoke to my nostrils and I hunched over, coughing and spitting phlegm. Chelle held my shoulders.

After a moment the fireman said, "We'll have our inspectors out at first light. They'll determine the cause. You have someplace to stay where we can contact you?"

"Next door." I gestured toward Chelle's house.

She gave him the phone number.

I took a last look at what had used to be my home. A skeleton rising against the sky, and a mound of steaming rubble. I stumbled, and Chelle steadied me.

Why? I thought. *How the hell did this happen?*

When we reached the steps to her house, I had to sit down. Trish, Chelle's mom, rushed out with an afghan and wrapped it around me. I clutched one of the banister posts and cried again.

My diplomas—high school and UC–Berkeley. The little box of photos and souvenirs from my former lovers. My favorite books. Records, tapes, and DVDs. Paperweights, now cracked or shattered. The bookends, two rabbits purchased at great cost by Hy, that supported my *Webster's Unabridged Dictionary*. The dictionary itself: I seldom used it any more, the Internet being quicker and easier, but sometimes I browsed through it, picking up esoteric lore.

How do you start over from a monumental loss like this?

I took a deep breath, leaned against Trish. All it did was pollute my lungs, and I coughed spasmodically.

Trish said to Chelle, "Go get my inhaler, please."

To me, she added, "I have asthma, and I think the inhaler will help you."

I thought: *Nothing will help me.* I said, "Thank you."

But the inhaler did help. After a few minutes I was breathing and thinking more or less clearly.

Chelle and Trish leaned against me, supporting me on either side. I said, "This fire was not a freak accident. It was arson."

A despicable crime that takes everyone and everything a person cherishes—sometimes her life.

"Why do you think that?"

"A former client—Daniel Winters—hired somebody to beat me up. The guy—Dixon Cooley—is in custody, but Winters is still at large."

"Why does this Winters have it in for you?" Chelle asked.

"I exposed him for insurance fraud. He went to prison, and it destroyed his career."

"Enough for him to want to kill you?"

"I don't know. I've made any number of worse enemies in the criminal world over the years."

Mother and daughter hugged me, but I finally looked at the still-smoking ruins of my house.

Rage was rising in me—the kind of fury I hadn't experienced in quite some time. It made my muscles go stiff, my teeth grind. A harsh metallic taste flooded my mouth.

Whoever had set this fire was going to pay dearly— through legal channels or otherwise.

Frankly, I preferred the possibilities of "otherwise."

7:11 a.m.

"I'll be home as soon as possible," Hy said.

RI had finally gotten through to him, and he'd called the Curleys' number immediately. The family hadn't been disturbed; they always rose early.

"Where are you?"

He hesitated. *Need-to-know basis.* Then he said, "Dubai."

"I'm not sure I even know where that is," I said. "Except that they've got the tallest building in the world or something."

His voice was strained with the same sadness and bitterness I was feeling. "Doesn't matter. The airport's good, and I've got buddies who can get me out quick on a fast plane."

"I love your buddies, Ripinsky. Someday we'll have to give a party for all of them."

"Only if we win the lottery and rent a stadium. But my buds and I stick together, just like you and I."

"Just like you and I."

7:30 a.m.

Trish brought me a cup of coffee, made soothing sounds, and sat down on the bed in their tiny guest room. "You feel like you can eat something?" she asked.

I shook my head.

"I'm so sorry about your house. But the cats are okay; they're in the kitchen eating as if they've never seen food before."

"I...I almost lost Jessie. She was under the bed, and I couldn't get her out. And I lost everything else." I started to cry again. Trish silently patted my arm.

Nothing about the previous night—or early morning— seemed real. But it didn't feel like a nightmare, either. Nightmares are easily recognized, are usually explained, and fade fast. Last night would never fade.

Rae arrived, bringing some of Mrs. Wellcome's—her housekeeper's—blueberry muffins. I refused one, and Trish left us to be alone for a while.

"Mick let me know what happened," Rae said. "He's as sick about this as I am."

"Nobody could be as sick as I am right now."

Rae sighed. "I can't dispute that. I want you and the beasts to come stay at our house."

"Thanks, but your puppy…" Rae and Ricky had recently adopted a little chocolate Lab.

"Frisk is gentle—he won't bother the cats."

"Okay, we'll come."

"Hy too. He's already on his way back from Dubai."

"How d'you know that?"

"I caught a film clip of him on the early news: he was trying to get onto a plane in Dubai, and apparently the press had heard about the fire, because they were bombarding him with questions—in Arabic, no less."

"Did he answer them?"

"Sort of."

So now my linguistically talented husband was mastering Arabic.

Rae said, "Shar, we've got to figure out how to handle this."

" 'We?' "

"I want you to appoint me as public relations director for the McCone Agency."

"Public relations—why on earth…?"

"The fire's all over the news; you're going to be hounded by the media—and not just those from the Bay Area. You don't need that, and I can run interference for you. I'm a good speaker, expert at evading a direct question, and a talented liar."

"You're a novelist."

"My latest book has been delivered. The next isn't due for a year and a half. And look at it this way—what are novelists but people who lie for a living?"

She had a point.

"So exactly what do I need you to do?" I asked.

"As I said, I'll run interference. While reports on ordinary house fires don't focus much on the residents' professional or personal lives, the stories on yours already have."

"Stories?"

"Various media outlets have been bombarded with messages accusing you of being allied with radical Muslims, terrorists, drug cartels...well, you know the lineup. They've described Hy as an ecoterrorist and insurgent."

I sat up, shaking free of my blanket.

"*Hy? Me?* They can't print crap like that, can they? It's libelous!"

"So far they've held off. But it's not exactly libelous because they'd be reporting on what information they've received, rather than what their opinion is. If the messages continue, they're bound to use them."

"And destroy our lives and careers. How do I stop this?"

"That's why you need me." She pulled a notebook from her purse. "First of all, I want to set up a press conference. Not with you or Hy there, but with me as your representative. Before they're even publicized, I'll brand those messages as a smear campaign. And I'll divulge as many of the details of the case you're currently working as you'll allow. Then I'll depict you as a martyr to somebody's guilt and fear. I'll ask for tips on whoever might've done this. And say that we aren't allowing them to intimidate us. It might flush whoever's behind this out of whatever cave they're hiding in."

"Jesus, overnight you've turned into a pit bull."

"It's been coming on for a long time, ever since the media did that number on Ricky and me when we hooked up. And I'm tougher than a pit bull; they can be great dogs if you train 'em right, but nobody's *ever* been able to train me."

No, no one ever had.

4:45 p.m.

The session with Rae had been intense. After she left I napped. She'd said she'd pick me up and take me to her house at five, but I was ready fifteen minutes early. The Curleys' house was silent, all of them going about their daily business, so I waited in the living room, which over-looked the street, but from which I couldn't see the ruins of my house. When Rae's car—a sleek red Jaguar—pulled up to the curb, I grabbed both cat cages that the Curleys had loaned me and hurried out.

Alex was shrieking. Jessie didn't make a sound. As Alex yowled all the way across town, I wondered what kind of cat was worse—a loudmouth or one you constantly had to check on to see if she was dead from shock.

Rae and Ricky's house was in Sea Cliff, an exclusive community above the Pacific south of the Golden Gate Bridge. Many of the homes were Spanish-style, stucco with red-tiled roofs; others were understated modern, with multiple stories scaling down the cliffs to the sea. Rae and Ricky's was one of the latter; I loved its spacious-ness and its views. But today I couldn't have cared less where I was.

A security guard motioned us through the tall iron

gates across the driveway. Over his years as a country music star, my former brother-in-law had been the victim of numerous celebrity stalkings, and he'd learned to take precautions.

We went in through the kitchen door, Alex's howls escalating. We set the cages down and looked at each other, shaking our heads. Mrs. Wellcome emerged from her quarters in a red sweat suit, her gray hair braided and hanging down her back.

"What on earth have you brought home?" she asked. "A creature from hell?"

"Actually he's a lovely cat," I told her. "But he hates being cooped up."

"I certainly can understand that." She went to the cage and opened the door. After a moment's hesitation, Alex crept out and into her arms. "That's all right, kitten," Mrs. Wellcome said, stroking him, "nobody likes to be put in jail." Alex quieted immediately.

I let Jessie out of her cage. She looked around expectantly: *Where's my food bowl?*

Mrs. Wellcome said, "I closed the door against Frisk. We'll need to introduce them gradually."

"Thank you," I told her. "I'll have to go out and get them litter boxes and food—"

"I took care of that after Ms. Kelleher called to say they were coming. They have everything they need, even toys." Her pale eyes brightened; she was going to enjoy playing with them.

"That's so good of you." I suddenly felt drained.

"Why don't you go upstairs and rest for a while?" Rae said. "I've got some calls to make."

"On the case, are you?"

She winked and said, "You bet."

I slipped between the sheets in the guest room suite, breathing in their sweet, clean scent. A long, hot shower and a toddy Rae had delivered to my door set me up for sleep.

As I drifted I thought not of the fire but of the many blessings in my life. Wonderful neighbors who had seen the flames and alerted the fire department, then cared for me. Wonderful friends like Rae and Ricky who had insisted on taking me and my cats in. Mrs. Wellcome providing for us. Family, for me, was not only blood relatives, but all the people with whom I'd bonded and grown throughout the years.

And Hy, who was at this moment rushing to be with me....

9:32 p.m.

"Hey, McCone."

Hy's breath and voice tickling my ear. I opened my eyes, rolled over, and looked up at him. His chin was stubbled, his eyes reddened, his hair tangled. Even in such a state, he was the most handsome man I'd seen in my life.

He gathered me into his arms, my head pressed to his shoulder. "It's going to be all right," he said. "Not the same, but all right."

I held him and my tears started to flow again. Jesus God, I thought, I was turning into the Vaillancourt Fountain. One of the ugliest pieces of spouting public art in the city, if not the whole country.

"I don't know what we'll do," I sobbed.

"We'll go on. You have any idea what caused the fire?"

"Arson."

"That an official finding?"

"No, but it's pretty damn clear to me."

"What makes it so clear?"

"First off, the elevator crash. Then two nights ago I was attacked by a thug hired by a disgruntled former client. The thug's now in custody, but who was there to stop the ex-client from hiring another to torch our house? And then there's the Warrick case: there must be any number of people who don't want that dug up. Plus a number of other cases over the years, where my work has aided the law in putting people away."

"Well, let's not get ahead of ourselves. Let the arson inspectors do their work first."

"I should hear from the fire department today or tomorrow at the latest."

"If it was arson, we'll get the son of a bitch responsible and make him pay—big-time. Take it into our own hands if we have to."

The determination in his voice stopped my tears. Hy and I could take on and had taken on a number of tough characters. We were a potentially lethal team, because we connected on so many levels.

"I'm with you," I said, "but in the meantime where will we live?"

"Well, we're in a pretty posh place right now."

"We can't stay with Rae and Ricky forever."

"There's the hospitality suite in the RI building, or our other safe houses around town."

RI maintained a number of innocuous locations—apartment buildings in the Sunset and Richmond districts, single-family homes on Bernal Heights and Potrero Hill—that were manned by their top-flight security people. High-risk clients were frequently housed in them until they could permanently be placed in safe locations.

"Since my agency's operating out of there, I'd prefer the RI building."

"Good." He reached for his phone and spoke to someone at his company. "They'll be getting it in shape right away."

"I'm glad you're close to public transit. My car burned up too."

"We'll get you another. A rental, in the interim."

"I loved that car. I loved our house." I started to cry again.

Hy pulled me closer. "We'll find another house. Or rebuild, only better."

"No. We can't replace..."

"McCone, cars and houses are just *things*. What's irreplaceable is life."

Yes, our lives, his and mine together. And those of our families and friends—

"Jesus!" I exclaimed. "Ma! If it's been all over the news—"

"Rae called everybody to reassure them that we're okay. I'm going to follow up with calls of my own. And now what I want you to do is take this pill and sleep some more."

"I've had enough pills in my life to stuff a camel."

"Bactrian or dromedary? One hump or two?"

I snorted. Then I laughed. Laughter—the source of healing.

As Hy handed me the pill I said, "I hope to hell I don't dream about camels."

SUNDAY, JANUARY 15

4:44 a.m.

When I woke, still in a half-drugged state, in Ricky and Rae's guest suite, I was alone. I put on one of the robes that hung in the closet and went into the adjoining sitting room. Hy was there, before the glowing embers in the small fireplace, working on his laptop.

"You sleep okay?" he asked.

"Yes. Whatever you gave me, it sure kills dreams."

"Yeah, I keep a supply on hand for the really bad times."

I knew about his really bad times, and they were far worse than my own. He'd toss and turn, mumbling to himself, then thrash about and cry out unintelligibly. I'd try to wake him, but sometimes he was so firmly in the throes of his nightmares that it took force to bring him out of them. Once he'd actually hit me on the jaw hard enough to leave a bruise before I'd subdued him.

I sat down beside him, put my head on his shoulder. "What're you working on?"

"Something you can't see." He shut the laptop.

"Need to know…"

"Need to know." He cradled my head in his hand.

Thank God he wasn't going to talk about linking our agencies again. My mind was not equipped to deal with complex issues at present.

"By the way," he said, "parts of Rae's press conference were on the eleven o'clock news last night. I DVRed it for you. She was pretty impressive."

"Unlike most multitalented people, she's impressive no matter what she does. When I think of the woman I originally hired...."

Rae had been working as a security guard when the head of the company referred her to me as an assistant. Although she was usually disheveled, more often late than not, and cowed by her perpetual-student husband who made her type all his papers, her enthusiasm and willingness to do the most routine of tasks compelled me to hire her. Within a year she'd shed the husband, created her own room in the attic of All Souls, and moved on with her life. There'd been some setbacks: a couple of disastrous relationships, a demand from her ex-husband for alimony when she began making good money—which was speedily dispatched in court, with Hank representing her. Since then her personal and professional trajectory had been upward.

"You want to watch the DVR?" Hy asked.

"Not now. I don't have an attention span." I closed my eyes, snuggling in closer to him. "In addition, I don't have any clothes. I don't have anything. I may never leave this house again."

"In your dreams. Rae's going to arrange for a personal shopper from that store you and she like to come out this morning. You're getting a whole new wardrobe."

"At great expense."

"The insurance will cover it."

"But all the other stuff that's gone—"

"A lot of it is, but not these." He reached into his pocket. "One of the firemen spotted that ammo box riveted to the linen closet floor and thought it must have had something to do with the explosion. He removed it, found your old thirty-eight Special and your grandma's garnet earrings."

He held up the earrings. The red stones sparkled in the light from the embers.

"Oh, Hy, thank you!"

"Don't thank me. Thank the fireman—whose name is Freeman—and the US Navy for making indestructible ammo boxes."

"I'll call Freeman in the morning, but not the navy. I doubt they'd approve of the use I put that box to."

9:10 a.m.

I'd slept another few hours. Now it was time to get moving—at least as much movement as a woman with only a bathrobe to wear can indulge in.

I phoned the office: Ted said that everybody was working on my house fire, trying to locate possible suspects in our case files. Next I called my insurance agent, who had heard about the fire and was full of sympathy—but, I sensed, already trying to wriggle out of paying off on the full amount of the policy. I then phoned Howard Freeman, the fireman who had saved my ammo box; he was pleased to hear from me but refused to take a reward. "All in a day's work, Ms. McCone." When I told him I wanted to contribute to one of their charities, he thanked me and recommended the Survivors' Fund.

Then I decided I was a survivor too and ought to get out of bed.

Mrs. Wellcome brought up a tray of pancakes, bacon, and fried eggs. Fortunately she couldn't know that shortly after I ate I threw it all up.

At ten thirty Rae's personal shopper arrived with trunks of clothing.

By the time she left at eleven thirty, I was the possessor of a small but attractive new wardrobe: all-new underwear; a robe in a handsome black-and-orange California poppy pattern; three pairs of jeans and five sweaters; a stylish all-purpose black pantsuit; three silk blouses; shoes, boots, and slippers; a warm tan woolen jacket and a black raincoat; a Baggallini purse; and a stunning low-cut red cocktail dress that exactly matched Grandma's garnet earrings. Other things—jewelry, scarves, miscellaneous accessories—could wait a while.

Rae then appeared, bearing such necessities of life as my brands of toothpaste and shampoo, a blow-dryer, a new brush and comb, face wipes and cotton balls, and a pint of peach ice cream, which we devoured on the spot. *That* I kept down.

While we were making pigs of ourselves, she said, "This reminds me of the time you and Hy were staying at the old RI building and that bomber blew it up. Remember: Julia had to go out and buy you almost everything."

"That wasn't nearly as bad. We were staying there because our house was under renovation. I still had plenty of stuff stored there."

"True." She scraped the last of the ice cream from her bowl. "So what do you think you and Hy will do?"

"For now we'll be staying at the RI hospitality suite—no way anybody's going to get at us there."

"Ricky and I had hoped you'd stay here."

"And we'd like to, but until this is all wrapped up, we don't want to put you two at risk. Or the kids, when they're here."

Her blue eyes darkened, and I knew she was thinking of various incidents of celebrity stalkings that had put both of them in danger. Such as the time she'd pulled Ricky off a stage in Albuquerque, New Mexico, when a man with a grudge was gunning for him.

I said, "By the way, I heard your press conference went well. Hy DVRed it, but I haven't had time to watch it yet."

"It wasn't bad. I darted and weaved here and there, confused the hell out of them until most of them decided it wasn't really much of a story. Now what can I do?"

"Well, I'll have to deal with the annoying little things: I'll need a new driver's license, investigator's credentials, credit cards, and cell phone. Fortunately I keep my important papers—passport, birth certificate, insurance policies, will, and property deeds—in the safe at the office. My three-fifty-seven, too. Hy's notified the Mendocino and Mono County sheriffs' departments that our places there might be at risk, but their departments cover a huge area and haven't the manpower to watch them full-time."

"You have caretakers, don't you?"

"Well, sure, but in Mono County he's the ranch manager and has lots of other things to tend to. In Mendocino the guy takes care of five other houses besides ours."

"Alarms connected with the fire and police and sheriffs' departments?"

"Now you're sounding like my insurance agent. Yes, we do, but you and I both know how easily such devices can be tampered with."

We sat in silence for a moment—both, I suppose, contemplating another pint of peach ice cream.

Rae said, "At least let me take care of the cell phone and credit cards; I might even be able to get you temporary driver's and pilot's and investigator's licenses."

"Don't you have other things to do?"

"Hell no. Like I told you, I'm not starting my next book till April. Ricky and I have no major travel plans till July. What am I supposed to do? Sit around and watch the fog drift by?"

"Then I accept your offer. But I'll owe you."

"Yeah, big-time." She grinned, her lightly freckled nose crinkling. "You can work some of it off by letting me come car shopping with you. Ricky always buys mine, and I know I'm a better bargainer than him. I also wouldn't mind helping you house-shop, if you do."

"Agreed."

Then the phone rang. Rae answered, whispered, "Your mother."

"Which one?"

"Saskia."

"Okay, I'll take it."

"Sharon, how are you?" her low voice asked.

"As well as possible under the circumstances. How did you know where to find me?"

"Hy gave me the number, and then I spoke with your other mother."

"How is Ma?"

"Calm. Frankly, I'm surprised. Her responses to other difficult situations have struck me as slightly hysterical."

"She wasn't always like that." I remembered Katie McCone, as she'd been called then, in her straw sun hat, digging with her bare hands in the dirt we'd filled the swimming pool with to grow vegetables after a sonic boom from a fighter plane out of NAS Miramar had irreparably cracked it.

"Well, maybe she's reverted to her former self, then. I'm glad Kay and I have become good friends over the years. Is there anything either of us can do?"

"I think the situation's under control—for now."

No sooner had I hung up than the phone rang again. Rae said, "You pick up this time."

"Daughter, is that you?" The familiar voice was harsh from a lifetime of smoking. Elwood Farmer, my birth father, who lived on the Flathead reservation in Montana. As with Saskia, I'd had no idea he existed until a few years ago.

"It's me," I said.

"This house fire—it was bad?"

"We lost everything."

"Saskia telephoned me, but she didn't know how bad at the time. She gave me this number. You weren't injured?"

"No. Even the cats got out okay."

"Then I will pray for you."

"Elwood—"

"As I have told you, you may call me Father."

"Okay, *Father*, but you know I'm not religious."

"Prayers are not hurtful things for those of us who believe to send out to those who don't."

The comment stung—which Elwood had intended it to do. "I'm sorry, Elwood... Father."

He said something in his native tongue and broke the connection. But the caring and comfort in those incomprehensible words from this relative stranger who had sired me filled me with strength.

The next call was from Hy: The RI hospitality suite was set up for us to move in. He'd sent one of the guards out for groceries. Rae volunteered to take my new things and the cats over there. I agreed, hoping to hear from Mick or one of my other operatives.

No calls. Mainly I sat in a chair overlooking the ocean and brooded.

Hy had said we could rebuild. But did I want to on the same lot, providing the insurance company forked over? I wasn't sure. I loved the neighborhood and the neighbors. I'd loved the house, but it would be impossible to replicate, and I couldn't imagine another structure standing in its place. The alternative was to sell the lot and, land values being what they were in the city, even in the current recession, I'd probably get a decent price. But then what?

A condo in one of those high-rises that were springing up like mushrooms in the rainy season? God, no. It was bad enough I'd be working out of the RI building. A house in Sea Cliff near Rae and Ricky? Hy and I could afford one, but the incessant fog would drive both of us crazy.

Pacific Heights? Maybe: the weather was usually good there. Nob Hill? Tel Hill? North Beach? Too congested. Potrero Hill? Bernal Heights? Maybe: they were also good-weather areas.

Trouble was, I couldn't get enthusiastic over any place.

Give it time, McCone. You're still grieving over the loss of your home.

If I hadn't been in the middle of this case, I'd've left and flown up to Touchstone or to the ranch in the high desert. Or driven either scenic route—

But I didn't have a car. Rae was taking care of a rental, as well as replacements for my driver's and investigator's and pilot's licenses, but I had no idea how long it would take. In the meantime, I didn't have anything—

Stop this pity party, McCone! You have photocopies of everything important in the office safe. Get off your ass and do something.

I got off my ass—and the phone rang again.

It was Rob Warrick; his voice sounded strange. Early this morning I'd asked Ted to call every current client, and all other persons connected with my cases, and give them this number.

He said he was so sorry to hear about the fire, then came to the point of his call.

"I just finished clearing everything out of Caro's storage unit, and I came across some papers and letters to her that might interest you. They were in an envelope taped to the back of that cabinet. Some of them look to be originals of the Xeroxes she tried to bring you the night she was attacked."

"And the letters?"

"Also originals, from an old friend of hers from high school named Valerie. They're all dated in August, but the year isn't specified, and there're no envelopes with a post-mark or a return address."

"Do you know this Valerie?"

"I never met her, but Caro talked about her a lot. I was under the impression that they'd fallen out of touch, though."

"What's Valerie's last name?"

"Benton? No—Benbow. That's it."

"And these letters say...?"

"They're kind of puzzling. I'd like to show them to you in person."

"Okay," I said, and gave him the address. "Have your ID ready for the security guard."

2:23 p.m.

When I opened the door to Rob Warrick, he seemed in-timidated by the premises. "Who lives here?" he asked.

"Relatives."

"Nice place, although that can't possibly make up for losing your home. What caused the fire?"

"The fire department called a few minutes ago. They're pretty sure it was arson. There was a charred gasoline can under the deck."

For a moment he didn't speak. Then he asked, "Because of Caro's case?"

"You have any reason to believe that?"

"No, although it *is* a coincidence."

"And you distrust coincidences."

"Yeah."

"So do I. By the way, how's Patty doing?"

"Mulching and composting with a vengeance—even in the rain."

"Her form of therapy, I guess. And you?"

"I'm doing okay. I thought I'd made sense of things, and then I found these."

He handed me a sheaf of newspaper clippings and letters handwritten on heavy bond paper.

"You recognize the handwriting?" I asked.

"No."

"Okay, let me read them." I led him into the living room, where four easy chairs overlooked the sea. "You relax—the bar's over there, the kitchen's through the door. Help yourself to whatever pleases you."

Rob helped himself to three fingers of Ricky's best single malt scotch and settled down in the chair beside me as I read.

August 2

Caro:

I know it's inexcusable, but what's done is done. And maybe, in its way, justice has been served, too. None of us likes this charade, but for Dave's sake we must go on with it. So much depends on preserving the status quo. What she did is reprehensible, and so, so unfair to you. But we must— and we will—go on.

Valerie

August 9

Caro:

I hate this as much as you do, and I wouldn't go on with it except for old times' sake. When he called and begged me to substitute, I couldn't refuse. Please believe me, it wasn't the money. It was the memory of the days when we were so close.

Valerie

August 30

Caro:

Finally we're all safe. I know how hard it's been on you, but now you're back in the fold—is that a sheepherding term? I never remember those things you've told me. Please join us and live easily. We await your arrival!

Valerie

"Not much to go on," Rob said.

"I don't know; Benbow's an unusual name. I'll have one of my employees start a trace on Valerie. The dates—August second, ninth, and then the thirtieth—make me wonder if there weren't more in between. This mention of sheepherding—that also interests me."

"I don't think Caro knew anything about sheep. Of course, I could be wrong."

I thought of the private investigator Edna Sheep; maybe her last name was why Caro had hired her before turning to Ham Roth. Sheep versus pigs. The idea was ridiculous. But sheep—there was something about them....

"Of course," I said, "Jethro Weatherford kept sheep."

"Who?"

"Doesn't matter right now." I stood. "I need to do some research. May I keep these letters?"

Rob stood too. "Certainly. And now I've got to get back to the office. I've been neglecting my work so much that I'm afraid they'll boot me out of the firm. Call me when you have something."

I walked him out, then went back to the living room and looked at the laptop Rae had loaned me.

Sheep. What the hell could sheepherding have to do with all of this?

4:07 p.m.

Apparently sheepherding had a lot to do with it, according to the Internet.

The Waldens had threatened Jethro Weatherford with a lawsuit over letting his sheep stray onto their land.

Jethro had responded, saying they'd better not set foot on his property.

Then the boundary dispute had started: the Waldens had claimed that a corner of Jethro's ranch actually belonged to them. A court had ruled otherwise. Over the next six months, four of Jethro's sheep had been brutally killed.

The Waldens had denied they'd had anything to do with the killings, but a nearby ranch hand taking a shortcut across Jethro's place said he'd seen an employee of Dave and Kayla's in the pasture around the times the animals had been slaughtered.

The Waldens, it seemed, were good at denial.

The phone rang and I let the call go to the machine, but when I heard Jim McCullough's voice I picked up.

The fireman said, "The suspect you mentioned who might've done your house fire, Daniel Winters, cleared out of his apartment yesterday afternoon. Was picked up on a DUI north of Sacramento. For once the Highway Patrol paid attention to our BOLOs."

"Did he confess?"

"No. Lawyered up with Iron Mike Falvey, but I doubt Mike'll be representing him much longer. He doesn't like clients who don't follow orders. Problem is, Winters has an alibi for the time of the arson: he stopped by at Capitol Casino in Sacramento, drank too much and made an ass of himself. Quite a few employees and patrons can identify him."

"Maybe distancing himself from another thug he'd hired to set the fire?"

"Possibly. But to be frank, I don't see him for the job. When his first thug failed, I doubt he tried another."

I sighed. "So he won't be charged for anything except drunk driving."

"Unfortunately, it's not against the law to be vicious and stupid."

After I ended the call, I read the Valerie letters again. With Winters out of the picture, it was all beginning to make sense. I strongly suspected who had set my home on fire, and I was determined to nail the bastard.

5:17 p.m.

None of my more experienced operatives were available: Craig and Adah were still down with the flu; Julia didn't answer her home or cell phone; Derek had gone to Las Vegas for the weekend; Patrick and Thelia weren't reachable either.

I knew that Mick didn't want to work outside the office any more, but he was my last hope. He picked up right away when I called him.

"Are you free? I need a ride and backup."

"For what?"

"I think I've figured this case out. But I need...well, you'll see."

"Does this involve me getting shot at, stabbed, or bludgeoned?"

"Not if I can help it. Do you happen to have a shovel?"

"A *shovel*? You don't need a shovel to stuff plants into containers on a balcony in this building."

"Never mind. I'll see if there's one here. Pick me up as soon as you can."

"Shar—"

I broke the connection and went to look for a shovel, found a large one in the gardening shed. Then I changed into my new heavy-duty boots and waited for Mick.

5:55 p.m.

Mick's car was an old blue Porsche that he'd bought for fifty cents from his father. In California, license plates remain with the vehicle unless the new owner decides to change them; the Porsche's read COBWEBS, the name Mick himself had suggested after Ricky's early big hit—"Cobwebs in the Attic of My Mind." The car required a lot of maintenance, and the plates attracted stares, but I supposed Mick kept it out of sentiment. Mainly he rode his Harley or drove Alison's car.

He got out and, when he saw the shovel, opened the trunk. I tossed it inside.

"Where're we going?" he asked.

"The Alexander Valley."

"You look really pissed about something. What's going on?"

"Not now. I have to think."

Traffic was light on the bridge—not surprising for a murky, dark evening. Even so, some tourists were out, walking across the span in rain slickers and heavy sweatshirts. Why, I wondered, did anyone come to San Francisco in January? Reduced airfares and lodging rates, I supposed. I'd have bet many of them returned home complaining that they didn't see why everybody raved about the city, but those who did rave had seen it on a clear, balmy day when even the grumpiest citizen smiled.

Traffic slowed at the Novato Narrows, where three lanes became two for a ten-mile stretch between Novato and Petaluma; traffic always backed up there and came to stop after stop, no matter what the time of day or night. There were no exits, except for the county landfill.

I'd been silent the whole ride, going over the facts, looking for any false assumptions. No, it was solid.

Occasionally Mick glanced at me, but he didn't speak either.

6:58 p.m.

We exited the freeway on Lytton Springs Road and drove through dark countryside into the Alexander Valley. Lights from the vineyard homes and wineries were misted; Mick turned on the car's fog lamps, but they didn't help much and he slowed to well below the speed limit.

I decided to test my theory on Mick. I said, "Somebody fatally injured Caro and stole papers that were incriminating to him or her. Somebody killed Jethro Weatherford. Somebody burned my house down in an attempt to kill me. What could be so valuable as to motivate crimes like that?"

"Money."

I shook my head, stared out the window at the dark hills. "That's part of it, but…"

"But what?"

"What's more valuable and permanent than anything else you can possess?"

"Gold?"

"Good answer. But there's something else. And far more precious than a commodity that you store in a bank vault and never visit."

"Children?"

"Another good answer. But think again."

"Land."

"How about land that conceals a secret?"

"Okay. But what...?"

"If I'm right, you'll soon find out. First place we're going is Hewette Vineyards, which supplies the Waldens' grapes. I think the old man who owns it knows more about them than he admitted to me."

7:44 p.m.

Russ Hewette looked surprised when he opened his door to us. There was a pause before he said, "Ms. McCone, whatever are you doing here at this hour?"

"May we come in?"

He frowned, then motioned us through the door and into a parlor.

I said, "This is my nephew, Mick Savage."

They shook hands.

"I'm afraid I haven't been candid with you," I added, and extended one of my cards. "I need to ask you more about the Waldens."

He studied it, squinting his pale eyes. "I thought you were a somewhat estranged friend of theirs."

"I'm sorry—it was a subterfuge, to get you to talk about them."

"I don't appreciate that."

"I'm sure you don't. Can we start over?"

He hesitated, not inviting us to sit down.

"Please, Mr. Hewette. This is important. Two people have already died—maybe more—because of them."

His face tightened, reflecting his conflicting emotions. "You lied to me before. How do I know you aren't now?"

"You don't. But if you wish, you can phone Inspector Devlin Fast at the San Francisco PD. He'll inform you about the circumstances of the deaths of Caro Warrick and Jake Green."

"Who're they?"

"They were both connected to the Waldens."

He rubbed his chin. "No, I guess I don't need to call any cop."

He sat down in an old lounge chair that looked as if he spent most of his time in it, and motioned Mick and me toward a sofa.

I said, "Tell me about Jethro Weatherford's sheep being killed."

"Well, it was a while ago. Coyotes, most people said; their natural habitat's being destroyed with all these new people building in the hills, so they search for food in places they normally wouldn't."

"Jethro thought the Waldens were behind it because he wouldn't sell him that corner of his land."

"Yeah, but Jethro bought more sheep, and so far nothing's happened to them."

"But something happened to Jethro."

A pause. "Well, that's a fact, isn't it?"

"Kayla Walden," I went on. "You told me you haven't seen her up close in two or three years."

"That's correct. Only from a distance, and not often."

"But you've seen Dave."

"Why, sure. In the fields, as I told you before."

"Have you heard of anything unusual or different about Kayla since you last had contact with her?"

He frowned, and after a moment said, "Well, she's apparently calmed down a lot."

"How so?"

"The first few years, she was kind of wild. She drank a lot and sometimes she'd start public arguments with Dave in Geyserville."

"You witnessed these?"

"Two of them. Heard about a few more."

"What did they argue about?"

"*She* argued; he just looked embarrassed and resigned. Mostly it was about the usual—he'd spent too much at the hardware store, when she couldn't afford to get her hair cut. You know. One time I came upon them in their car, pulled off the road, practically in the ditch. She was yelling that she'd kill him and that woman if he didn't end it. Sounded to me as if Dave was getting something on the side. Friend of mine heard her screaming about killing herself after Dave had dragged her out of Kelso's Bar. After that I think that Dave must've gotten her into therapy or even an institution, because all the ruckus stopped—and it's been quiet ever since."

I pictured the attractive, pleasant Kayla I'd met at the winery. No way would she carry on like that.

"Mr. Hewette, is there any possible reason for you to think that the woman over there not might be Kayla Walden?"

"Of course she's Kayla. Same hair, same fondness for capes."

I remembered Amelia Bettencourt's claims that she was being followed by someone in a black cape. "So nothing's changed in the years the Waldens have lived next door to you?"

He considered for a moment. "Well…her bread."

"Her bread?"

"The bread she used to deliver every morning. She'd bring it to the door and knock, sometimes come in and have a slice with me. Now she just sends a loaf with one of the winery workers. You're going to think this is an old man's fancy, but it's not the same. The bread she used to bring me had a certain lightness, a quality…Oh, I can't describe it."

Mick said, "Like Grandma's. No one's home-baked bread is the same as anybody else's."

"Right," Hewette said. "Kayla's bread changed."

"When?" I asked.

"Maybe two, two and a half years ago."

Who would think that a case could turn on such a point as bread hot from the oven?

8:10 p.m.

We were standing in the grove of eucalyptus on Jethro Weatherford's property, my flashlight shining on ground littered with leaves and seedpods. It was even darker here than on the road, and the mentholated odor of the trees clogged my nostrils. The rustle of a few night birds was the only sound except for our breathing, and a chill wind blew the fog down from the coastal hills.

"Where do I dig?" Mick asked.

"Here, at the corner of the property."

He went at it, working steadily, muscles flexing, as I held the flashlight on the spot. It was a long time before the shovel clanged on metal and he stopped. "I think I've hit that drainage pipe."

"Good." I began to pace off the four-and-some yards that Nina Weatherford had drawn on the cocktail napkin. "The opening to it must be right around here."

Mick made a growling noise. "Why didn't you tell me to dig there in the first place?"

"I had to be sure."

He moved and began digging again. After a moment he grumbled, "You didn't need me for backup. A man with an aching back is more like it."

He flung more earth over his shoulder, and I could've sworn he was trying to scatter it over me, but I didn't complain. Frankly, I didn't blame him.

After several more minutes he said, "I think I've found the end of the drainage pipe," he said. "I'm gonna go down and clear it."

He dropped into the hole he'd made, and I heard him grunting as he pushed the earth around.

When he spoke again, his voice was strained. "Shar, there's something blocking this pipe."

"What is it?"

"Looks like an aluminum wine cask."

"Can you get it out of there?"

"I don't know." More grunts and a scraping noise. "It's really heavy."

"Can you boost it up here?"

"No way. It's heavy as hell. Must be full of rocks or something."

Not rocks. Human remains.

The true Kayla Walden. The one with the trust fund that couldn't be altered. The wife Dave Walden had replaced with someone named Valerie.

Dave Walden: the man who'd killed Caro on my front steps; the man who'd set my house on fire.

The fury that had been simmering in my gut spread through my entire body; my skin felt hot, then cold, then hot again. There was a faint roaring sound in my ears as I pulled my .357 from my bag.

"Shar?" Mick said. "What're you doing?"

I didn't answer, just started walking toward the road.

"Shar?"

"Call the county sheriff's department."

"But, Shar...?"

"I'm going up there to get the son of a bitch who torched my home and tried to kill me."

"Shar!"

I kept going.

10:01 p.m.

I was so angry that I didn't take a circuitous route to the Walden house—just stomped up the driveway, past the tasting room, to the front door. The lights inside were muted, Walden and Valerie already in bed, maybe.

Some internal governor told me to calm down, think

this through before I acted. I switched it off and pounded on the door.

Silence. Then shuffling sounds. As the knob turned, I raised the .357.

Dave Walden's face looked out over the security chain. He registered surprise when he saw the gun, then tried to shut the door. Savagely, I kicked it open, breaking the chain. He stumbled back, caught himself, started toward me. I pointed the gun at his head, my finger tight on the trigger. That stopped him. I stepped into the house, shut the door behind me.

"What the hell's the idea—?"

"Shut up, you bastard. Where's Valerie?"

"Who?"

"You know damn well who she is. The ringer you brought in to replace Kayla."

"I don't know what you're talking about—"

"I found the wine keg where you buried it beyond the drainage ditch. And we both know what's inside it. A simple DNA test on the real Kayla's remains…"

Fear twisted his features. I saw his body tense; he took another step toward me.

"Stand still!"

"You won't use that gun," he said.

"Try me."

Walden stopped again, jammed his hands against the sides of his head as if he were trying to crush it. "I didn't kill Kayla, she killed herself. All I did was hide her body in that keg."

"How did she kill herself?"

"Gunshot. She was always unstable, showed suicidal

tendencies. Finding out about my affair with Amelia put her over the top."

I half believed him. "How'd she find out?"

"Followed me. Then followed Amelia. She shot Amelia, but she couldn't live with what she'd done."

"So when you found her dead you put her body in the cask and brought in Valerie so you could continue bene-fitting from Kayla's trust fund. Who is Valerie?"

"An old friend of Caro's and Amelia's from school. She was hard up, had just gone through a divorce and lost her job. I thought of her because she really resembles Kayla."

"Where is Valerie now?"

He moved his hands in a helpless gesture. "I don't know. She took off after your first visit. The threat of exposure wasn't worth the money I'd given her, she said."

"The threat of being accessory to murder, you mean. Did Valerie know you killed Caro when she called you about the letters from Amelia she'd found, and said she was taking them to me?"

"No, Valerie didn't know anything about that. And that's not how it was, anyway. Caro tried to sell the letters to me. She gave me twenty-four hours to come up with a hundred thousand dollars, and said if I didn't she'd take them to you. As if I could get my hands on that kind of money! I drove down to the city and followed her. I didn't mean to kill her, I just wanted to get those letters out of her hands. She fought me, the envelope tore and the pa-pers blew all over. A car was coming up the street, so I grabbed what papers I could and ran."

"But not before you bludgeoned her."

"I didn't mean to!"

They never mean to kill their victims.

And Caro probably hadn't thought she was doing anything wrong in attempting to sell the letters. In fact, she'd felt entitled; her stupid, greedy blackmail attempt was her last chance to grab the brass ring that had eluded her all her life.

"So you got the evidence. I was no threat to you any more."

"I didn't know what the papers I lost were or how much Caro'd told you. And then you showed up here, asking about my connection to her, talking to that old drunken geezer, Weatherford. I saw your car at Russ Hewette's place too. You were getting too close. I had to do something."

"Yeah, you fucking piece of shit, you set fire to my house."

Panic surged in him, made him reckless. He lunged sideways, grabbed a table lamp and started to swing it at my head. I had no choice then—I shot him in the thigh.

He collapsed, clutching his leg and rolling around in pain, cursing me between groans and sobs.

I looked down at him, hating him and asking myself why I hadn't shot to kill.

Because I'm done with killing. It's too much of a drain on my spirit, my soul, whatever that thing is that supposedly lives inside all of us.

MONDAY, JANUARY 16

3:00 p.m.

M y parents," Rob Warrick said, "are unavailable— once again."

He, Patty, and I were seated around the oak table in the conference room next to my office in the RI building. The table was a treasure from the days when it had sat by the window in the All Souls kitchen—the site of card and board games, friendships, agony, soul-searching, and— occasionally—love. Unlike my chair, it would never be re- furbished; too much of our lives had gone into its scars and stains.

I wasn't surprised that Betsy and Ben had declined to attend this meeting, but I asked, "What was their excuse this time?"

"That Caro had ruined their lives anyway, and they didn't want to hear how you'd exonerated her once and for all of Amelia's murder. Besides," he added with a wry twist of his lips, "they're off on a tour of China."

I glanced at Patty, saw the hint of a smile. Maybe now, with the help of her brother—who had decided to move in with her and see that she took care of herself—she might eventually learn to laugh.

Rob asked, "You talk with the authorities up in Sonoma County?"

"Yes, they confirmed that they'd found human remains in the wine barrel and would be performing forensics tests to make sure they were of the real Kayla Walden."

"God." He shuddered. "That's got to be the ultimate in disrespect—putting your wife's body in a wine barrel and burying it in a drainage ditch. Does ATF think Walden killed Green too?"

"I'm not exactly in their confidence but no, I doubt it. One of their agents did tell me they apprehended the men who searched Jake Green's home while Mick and I were there. They were partners in his arms-smuggling scheme. Green had held out a key piece of equipment from them— a sophisticated type of detonator—but wherever he was keeping it, it wasn't in the house."

"But they didn't kill Green; he was already dead when they got there."

"Right. Green was probably killed by somebody else involved in one of his illegal schemes. They'll eventually find out who it was."

Maybe. Or maybe not. Doesn't really matter. Whoever killed Jake Green did the world a favor.

TUESDAY, JANUARY 17

1:43 p.m.

"Here's a place that looks interesting," Hy said.

"Hmmm?" We were taking a day off: we'd slept late and now were reading last Sunday's newspaper in bed at the RI hospitality suite; he was into the house ads and I was into the car ads.

"Victorian home, Noe Valley."

"Where in Noe Valley?"

"Twenty-Fourth Street."

"Garage?"

"Um...no."

"Too congested for on-street parking."

"Right."

I asked, "What do you think of a Corvette?"

"Too low-slung. They ride like skateboards. It'd ruin our spines."

"Yeah, and when the fiberglass shatters, you're looking at huge repair bills."

"Another BMW?" he suggested.

"Maybe, but I don't like the new ones as much as the

one I had, and I do want a brand-new car. Something sporty and fun to drive, before I get too old to enjoy it."

"You'll *never* get too old for that."

The phone rang, and I picked up. Deputy Ortiz in Sonoma County. He said they'd begun testing on the human remains in the wine barrel and had come up with preliminary evidence that they were Kayla Walden's, based on dental records and jewelry. DNA testing to confirm the identification would take longer.

"What?" Hy asked when I hung up.

"The remains in the wine barrel apparently are Kayla Walden's."

"What about this Valerie Benbow? Have they located her?"

"Not yet, and neither has Mick. She's probably going under a different name in a different part of the country by now. But eventually they will. She'll testify against Walden and get off with a slap on the wrist. In a way, I feel sorry for her."

"Why?"

"She's one of these small-time con artists who thought she had a toe through the door into the good life, probably imagined she could charm Dave Walden, but his kind aren't susceptible to being enchanted."

"Well, greed drives people to stranger acts than that. Like Walden: he would've lost everything under the terms of Kayla's trust."

After a moment I said, "There's still a problem about a highly sophisticated detonator belonging to Green that's gone missing."

"I don't think you have to worry about that."

"Oh?"

"It's been in my office safe since the day after Green died. Mick gave it to me."

"He found it?"

"Yeah, while you were upstairs in Green's house. It was in the basement room where the firearms were."

I recalled my nephew holding up something that looked like a flash drive for a computer and saying, *Decoding device. Something I whipped up in my spare time.*

"So he didn't actually have this creation that unlocks security systems?"

"Sure he does. But most of that stuff he can do on his own."

"The little shit! Why wouldn't he tell me?"

"He suspected what it was and was afraid that if he gave it to you, you might set it off."

"But why didn't you tell me?"

"Because nobody in my organization really knows how it works, any more than Mick does. We're holding it for the feds—who probably won't know either."

"God. I probably *would've* set it off. I'm sorry I called Mick a little shit—don't tell him."

"My lips are sealed with duct tape."

We both contemplated our want ads in silence for a moment.

"You know," I said, "there's a real irony in this case."

"What's that?"

"It all centered around the issue of gun control, yet in the end I had to use my gun to stop Walden."

"But you used it responsibly, in self-defense. People

who are empowered by the law to carry guns for professional reasons—"

"Aren't always responsible. The federal probe last year of the cops who were using their exemptions to buy assault weapons for resale to arms dealers proved that."

"The probe resulted in crackdowns. Slowly, we're gaining ground."

"Too slowly for me."

Hy went back to the want ads. After a moment he said, "Now here's a property for us: Lake Street, corner lot, three stories, exceptional details. Brown-shingled. I know you love brown shingles."

"Mark it," I told him. "You know, the Mercedes S-Class models look good."

"Pricey, though."

"Not really. You should see what they're asking for one of those asshole-creating machines."

"Porsches? You'd never buy one, anyway."

We continued perusing the ads.

Hy said, "Here's an even better one. Another corner lot, but in the Marina. Two stories, four bedrooms, three baths, two-car garage, quiet block."

"I've always loved the Marina, but think what happened there during Loma Prieta."

The October 17, 1989, quake, measuring a major 6.9 on the Richter scale, had toppled many residences in the Marina, and the ensuing fires from broken gas lines had swept through the district.

"Could happen anyplace in the city," Hy said. "Anyplace in the country. Hell, they just had a big quake in

Indiana. No point in spending your life worrying about the what-ifs."

"You're right, no point at all." Homes in the Marina had been rebuilt, retrofitted against another disaster. Other precautions—utility systems, home foundations, fire department response times, and seismic monitoring—had been upgraded.

I looked back at the car ads: Audi, Chevrolet, Nissan, Toyota, Volvo... All models of all makes were making me crazy. I dropped the pages to the floor.

"McCone, this house is open today from two till five."

"Is it affordable?"

"Yes."

"Four bedrooms. One for us, two for our offices, one for guests. Is there a picture?"

He showed me.

"Too grainy. Can you pull it up on the laptop?"

He did. "Oh, yes, it's great," he said as he passed the machine over to me.

Spanish style, red-tiled roof. Hardwood floors and fireplaces. Newly remodeled kitchen and bathrooms. A pretty landscaped backyard with a garden gnome. Usually I hate them, but I could see myself sticking a Santa cap and glittery garland around it at Christmastime.

I said, "Two to five. Let's get up, go out to brunch, and take a look at it."

He turned to me and smiled. "This reminds me of when I changed the plane's course for Reno and we got married."

"It's much the same—a turning point."